GRANT J TRAINER
Order of Solomon

Copyright © 2025 by Grant J Trainer

All rights reserved. No part of this publication may be reproduced, stored or transmitted in any form or by any means, electronic, mechanical, photocopying, recording, scanning, or otherwise without written permission from the publisher. It is illegal to copy this book, post it to a website, or distribute it by any other means without permission.

This novel is entirely a work of fiction. The names, characters and incidents portrayed in it are the work of the author's imagination. Any resemblance to actual persons, living or dead, events or localities is entirely coincidental.

Designations used by companies to distinguish their products are often claimed as trademarks. All brand names and product names used in this book and on its cover are trade names, service marks, trademarks and registered trademarks of their respective owners. The publishers and the book are not associated with any product or vendor mentioned in this book. None of the companies referenced within the book have endorsed the book.

First edition

This book was professionally typeset on Reedsy.
Find out more at reedsy.com

For
Katherine, Noah, Lily and Jacob

Acknowledgments

Thank you to everyone who has helped and supported me in writing this book. To my friends who have listened to me bounce ideas around or listen to me tell them all the different versions of this book.

To Stephen who helped me do more than I thought I did.

To Adriana and Gordon, who read drafts and gave me the best feedback possible, you are a part of this book.

Listening to movie scores gave this book a soundtrack in my head.

Thank you.

Chapter 1

He feels the sun on his face as he walks up the ramp into the open air. The heat clings to his body, making his bare chest sweat. The roar of the crowd swells as they see their champion, the gladiator they have been longing for. He looks down at his sword, gifted to him by Caesar himself, a symbolic gesture to mask the fact that he is still a slave, a tool for entertainment and death. The sword gleams under the sun, but to him, it's no more than a shackle, a reminder that even his victories serve another's whims. He smiles at how absurd it makes this boy king of Rome seem. He has known rulers like him all his life, each hiding weakness behind the veil of power.

Pushing his thoughts aside, he kneels and drives the sword into the sand. The sound of the blade piercing the earth is swallowed by the cheers. For them, this is a spectacle, but for him, it is survival. The crowd always loves a show, so he grabs a handful of sand, rubbing the grains onto his chest, and gives the crowd a brief glance. Their cheers rise, so he stands, lifts the sword, and thrusts it into the air. He doesn't need to look to know their faces, desperate for blood, eager for death. They don't care whose. The taste of death lingers as he prepares for what is to come.

He wakes with a jolt, as he always does, dream and reality tangled together. His head still foggy, he questions which is real, the dream or this moment. He touches his chest as if expecting to feel the grit of sand, but there's only the worn fabric of his shirt.

Sitting in the front seat of the stolen car, he adjusts the seat, sitting straighter. He coughs and looks around, trying to get his bearings. His rumpled clothes cling to him, stiff from sleep. The fabric smells faintly of sweat and gasoline, grounding him in the present, no matter how much he wants to escape it. He rubs his face with both hands, feeling his rough, dirty skin against the stubble on his ageing face. Outside, everything is still, just darkness. The world feels forgotten, abandoned like the car he sits in.

He sniffs, wipes his nose on his sleeve, and twists the screwdriver jammed into the ignition. The old car sputters to life, black smoke curling from the exhaust before it dies again. The failure feels almost poetic, as if the car understands the weight of his exhaustion. He tries once more, and after a long, agonising moment, the engine finally comes to life and stays running. The sound is rough, uneven, but persistent, much like his own heartbeat.

Slowly, the car moves forward, leaving the memory of the dream behind, or maybe carrying it with him, hidden in the depths of his mind, begging to resurface.

Chapter 2

Four Park View looks like every other house on the quiet street, just a few miles from the capital. Built in the late 1990s, each has a modest back garden, a single-car garage, and a shed. The street is dimly lit as heavy rain obscures the streetlights, falling in sheets as the wind picks up. Thunder rumbles through the clouds, drawing closer.

Inside number 4, the only light comes from the blue bulbs of electronic flycatchers mounted on the walls of every downstairs room. Beneath them, bowls sit nearly full of an unusually high number of flies, drawn to the light. The smell in the house is strong, a mix of perfume, aftershave, and cleaning products trying to mask the overwhelming stench of death.

Another light comes from the open fridge, where the man once known as Phil Jones stands, staring inside. He still finds it astonishing what humans eat. The fridge is stocked to maintain appearances, but most of the food is long past its sell-by date. He picks up a bottle of milk, shakes it to stir the thickening liquid inside, and stares at it.

His gaze drops to a wet puddle on the floor, and he tilts his head, following it toward the back door. Phil tenses when he sees the lock has been broken from the outside.

"You really need to go shopping. That food's way past its sell-by date."

The voice startles Phil, and he drops the milk bottle. It shatters on the tiles, glass and milk spilling everywhere. Light from the fridge spills out, casting a faint glow over the figure in the doorway, casually examining a rotten apple. Phil stands, momentarily confused.

James leans against the doorway between the kitchen and dining room, his broad frame filling the space. His slept-in long coat and clothes are as wet and dirty as his body. A confident, cheeky smile plays on his rugged, chiselled face—a face of a man whose haunted dreams have deprived him of a proper sleep for years. Before Phil can react, James throws the apple and sprints toward him.

Phil is distracted by the apple flying toward him, tilting his head to dodge it just as James slams into him, driving his knee into Phil's gut and sending him crashing into the fridge. Before Phil can react, James yanks the fridge door wider and kicks him in the face, breaking his nose. The fridge topples over, crashing down on top of him.

Phil wakes up and tries to stand, but he can't. His arms, ankles, and torso are bound tightly to a chair, the barb wire cutting into his skin, causing searing pain. He attempts to shout, but his mouth is sealed shut with tape. A wet, thumping sound reaches

CHAPTER 2

his ears from the left, along with the sound of a man exerting himself. Straining his neck, he turns to see his wife, Susan, lying on the dining table. Her arms and legs are stretched out, bound to the table legs with the same barbed wire that holds him. Her head hangs off the edge, directly in front of him.

The man, James, is standing over her, delivering punch after punch to her face and body, only pausing to catch his breath. Susan's face, hair, and pyjamas are soaked in her own blood, a thick puddle pooling on the floor beneath her. Her face is so badly swollen and cut that Phil can no longer recognize her. He glances past Susan to see their two daughters, 17-year-old Tracey and 15-year-old Suzanne, tied to chairs on the other side of the room. Their mouths are covered with the same tape that seals his own.

"Show yourself, you son of a bitch!" James screams into Susan's face, spittle spraying her. He punches her again, her limp body taking the blow in silence, she's unconscious.

"Stop hiding. He told me, the female of the house." James pleads, his voice filled with frustration.

He reaches behind his back and pulls out a SIG Sauer P229 from a holster on his belt.

"I don't have time for this, and I need you to show yourself."

James strikes Susan's jaw with the pistol, the crack of bone unmistakable. Her jaw snaps, but still, she doesn't make a sound.

"This is just a waste of time. These poor kids you've turned into puppets have suffered enough."

He presses the gun against Susan's temple. Her eyes flutter open, wide with terror. If her jaw weren't shattered, she might have screamed.

"I'm not even going to count to three," James says, his voice low.

Without hesitation, he pulls the trigger. A thunderous bang fills the room, and a hole tears through the back of Susan's head, the bullet embedding itself in the floor. Muffled screams come from the other three. James steps back, wiping sweat from his brow, and scratches his temple with the hot muzzle of the gun, flinching from the heat. But something is wrong, Susan remains motionless, and it confuses him.

He walks to a sideboard and picks up a letter, reading the address aloud.

"Number 4."

James pauses, suddenly aware of the silence in the room. The muffled screams have stopped. Slowly, he turns to face the family. Phil sits still in his chair, staring directly at James, his eyes vacant and unblinking. Motionless.

James looks at the girls. Tracey mirrors Phil's blank stare, but Suzanne, she's different. Her body is slumped forward, head bowed toward the floor, where a pile of torn tape lies at her

CHAPTER 2

feet.

Muffled laughter comes from behind Suzanne's gag as her body begins to contort and stretch in the chair. The sound of bones cracking echoes through the room as her limbs extend, growing into grotesquely long arms and legs. Her head tilts back, and the tape covering her mouth falls away, revealing an enormous, deformed Cheshire-like grin. Suzanne lifts her forefinger, now grotesquely elongated, the bone having burst through the skin, with a sharp nail twice as long as her face. She rips off the remaining tape, tearing away parts of her lips and left cheek. The smile widens, her cheeks splitting open to reveal rows of shark-like teeth. Her eyes are now fully black, wide and menacing.

Pointing her torn finger at James, she speaks, her voice raspy and screeching, like nails on a blackboard.

"So, you're the one causing all this panic. You're the one they talk about."

She glances at Susan, lifeless on the table, and lets out a chilling laugh.

"What a waste."

Her smile deepens. "Ready?"

"Oh, boll—" James mutters, but before he can finish, Suzanne launches herself at him. The force of her impact is beyond anything her size should deliver. Each blow to his abdomen shatters ribs, and then she snaps his collarbone. The momentum sends them crashing through the wall into the living room, James hitting the ground hard. His shoulder dislocates as Suzanne claws at him with vicious speed, her long, sharp nails ripping through his skin and muscle. Blood splatters everywhere, covering them both.

With his right hand, James pushes her face away, managing to bring his knee up and kick her off. Suzanne stumbles back, giving him a moment to roll to the side and jump to his feet. He runs through the door and into the hall, stumbling up the stairs. Racing into a bedroom, he slams the door shut behind him.

"Not going the way you wanted, human? Catching your breath won't stop your insides from falling out." Suzanne screeches, her voice echoing through the house.

James clutches his left shoulder, blood streaming down his arm. He tips the wardrobe over, blocking the door, and glances toward the window as the banging on the door starts. Bracing himself, he prepares to dive through the glass, but then everything goes silent.

Panting, he looks down at his body, noticing the deep claw marks on his torso. Without understanding how or why, a familiar heat courses through him. His wounds begin to close rapidly. The gashes turn to scars, his shattered ribs and collarbone burn as they fuse back together, and the bleeding stops. He wipes the sweat from his brow, no longer needing distance to heal.

CHAPTER 2

Being near a monster always speeds up his healing, but why?

Before James can process his thoughts, Phil crashes through the door, slamming into him. James struggles to block the frenzied blows raining down on his face as a berserker-like Phil lashes out. Grabbing Phil by the ears, James spins and lifts him off the floor, but Phil's head detaches from his ears, sending him crashing into the wall. Without waiting for Phil to recover, James grabs a dresser and smashes it into Phil's face. Not hesitating, he bolts out of the room and down the stairs, knowing he needs to escape and regroup.

Suzanne's high-pitched screech echoes through the house, her voice almost sing-song. "Not going the way you'd hoped, is it?"

A low, rumbling laugh underlines her words as she continues. "We've heard about Manchester last month, the man with no name, hunting us for years. But what a waste. Killing monsters, thinking you were stopping us."

James pauses at the bottom of the stairs, her words striking deep.

"So, what took you from your flock, what drove you apart?" Suzanne taunts.

James turns to look up the stairs, where Phil now stands. His face is in pieces, his body mangled, but still, he stands. For years, James has tracked these monsters, thinking he was killing them, only to realize now, they don't die. His memories, tangled and fragmented, provide no clue to his past. For 50 years, he's followed an instinct to hunt them down, with no explanation as to why he doesn't age, why he can't die. He thought he was doing good, but now it feels like a lie.

A rage unlike anything James has ever felt surges within him. He lets out a guttural roar, losing control. Turning toward the dining room, he sees a deformed Tracey standing in the doorway. He charges at her, kicking her back into the room. As he moves in for another strike, Phil leaps onto his back. It doesn't slow him, James grabs Phil, flips him over his shoulder, and slams him against the wall.

Tracey is on him next, grabbing his hair and stabbing her sharp claws deep into his body, piercing internal organs. James gurgles in pain as she throws him through the hole in the wall, crashing into the living room. His body slams into the floor with a sickening crack, bones fracturing from the impact. Fighting through the pain, he twists his left arm back into place, spits blood, and forces himself to his feet, ready for the next attack.

It doesn't take long. Tracey charges at him with unnatural speed. In a single motion, James sidesteps and slashes her throat with a knife from his belt. She crashes into the wall, clutching her neck, flailing silently as blood pours from the wound. Without hesitation, James thrusts the knife into the top of her skull, ending her struggle.

Phil leaps onto him again, and James, still holding the knife embedded in Tracey's head, crashes to the floor. Phil's claws

CHAPTER 2

tear into his arms and face, ripping flesh and chipping bone. One strike catches James' left eye, ripping it from the socket.

Through the pain, James manages to grab Phil by the neck, pulling him close, and bites hard into Phil's face. Rolling away, James pushes himself to his feet, wiping the blood from his eye socket and spitting out Phil's flesh.

"Bet that hurt." James taunts, breathless but defiant.

Phil lunges at him, grabbing James by the throat and pulling him close.

"You tell me." Phil growls, his voice no longer entirely his own. Suzanne's voice echoes from outside the room.

Phil drives his clawed hand deep into James' stomach. Gritting his teeth, James jerks his head back, then slams it into Phil's face, nearly crushing it. The fight is dragging on longer than James expected, and something is shifting inside him, an unfamiliar sensation he's never experienced before. His body burns as it heals, but now, there's a new heat, more concentrated and intense, radiating from his forearms.

Holding onto Phil, James notices a strange white glow seeping through the torn fabric of his sleeves. Stunned, he releases Phil and stumbles backward, rolling up his sleeves to reveal glowing, circular markings etched into his skin. The white light pulses like a mixture of electricity and fire, and the burning sensation gives way to an exhilarating tingling that courses through his entire body. The glow intensifies.

Suddenly, the room is filled with a blinding flash as a car crashes through the living room window, flinging both James and Phil across the room. The car skids to a stop, half of it sticking out of the house, smoke rising from the bonnet. One headlight is shattered, casting a dim light across the chaotic room. Suzanne drops from the ceiling, her claws digging in as she lands on the car's bonnet, causing the engine to sputter and die. With unnatural strength, she rips the windscreen off. The car is empty.

Suzanne surveys the room just as Tracey's head explodes, sending blood and gore flying everywhere. Her body crumples to the floor, lifeless.

Standing in the doorway is a woman called Helen, her figure strong and commanding, holding a Remington 870 DM semi-automatic shotgun where Tracey's head once was. She breathes heavily, blood running down her face. Her long red curls are matted with blood and dust, and her long coat is dirty and torn.

James, still on the ground, covered in blood, stares at her in shock. His body has almost fully healed, his eye has regenerated, and the deep gouges in his face and arms have closed, leaving only faint scratches. The holes in his stomach no longer bleed. The white light has faded, leaving black tattoo-like markings where it once glowed. He slowly looks from his arms to the woman standing before him. There's something deep within him, a feeling in his gut, he knows her.

"What?" he whispers, barely audible, but his mind is certain.

CHAPTER 2

She locks eyes with him, her expression a mixture of disbelief and recognition.

"James?" she says flatly, as if testing the sound of his name.

Before he can respond, Helen interrupts, her voice tinged with shock. "You know me?"

They turn toward the car. Suzanne, crouching on its roof, is no longer the same monstrous figure. Her skin is peeling away, revealing bone and muscle beneath. Despite her grotesque appearance, her eyes betray something unexpected - fear.

"Don't move," Helen orders, her gaze locked on Suzanne, not sparing a glance at James.

Suzanne barely registers what's happening until the third strike slams into her body, sending her flying backward into the wall. Her insides rupture from the impact. Helen follows up, smashing her elbow into Suzanne's left eye socket, cracking it. Without hesitation, she grabs Suzanne by both arms, spins her around, and hurls her through the living room wall into the kitchen. Suzanne crashes to the ground, skidding across the floor until she collides with the back door.

Helen leaps through the hole in the wall after her, drawing two SIG Sauer P229s from the holsters on her hips. She aims at Suzanne's face and fires three bursts from each gun. Suzanne instinctively raises her hands and squeezes her eyes shut. When she dares to open them, she sees the bullet holes in the floor in front of her but not in her.

James enters the dining room slowly, wiping blood and dust from his face with a cloth. All the injuries he had sustained, scrapes, slashes, gouges, are gone. He watches Helen, unsure of what to ask first.

"You called me James. How do you know me?"

Helen turns, holstering her guns, her brows furrowed in confusion. She ignores the question, focusing back on Suzanne, who still hasn't moved.

"From your setup here and your laughable excuse for security, I'm guessing you're a Marquise, but not just that, you and your lot are sleepers. Keeping a low profile, trying not to draw attention, but you couldn't resist could you. Setting up an online page for swinger parties. The whole pig you ordered from the butcher for tomorrow night's event tipped me off. Your indulgence made you sloppy, and now here I am."

Suzanne stays silent, her large black eyes shifting from Helen to James and back again. Panic flickers in them. This unknown man, James, has been waging a personal war for years, but no one had ever identified him. How could someone so feared remain a mystery? For centuries, Suzanne had heard whispers of James and Helen, their names shifting over time but their legend remaining the same. James was supposed to be dead, the first of their kind to fall, a fatal mistake never reported.

Helen crouches in front of Suzanne, pressing the barrel of her shotgun against Suzanne's face. "I'm going to stop you right there."

CHAPTER 2

Can she read Suzanne's thoughts?

"No, I can't read your mind," Helen continues, as if answering an unspoken question.

"But I can see what you're thinking through those big, empty eyes. I'm just as surprised as you are to see James here, but don't think that gives you any advantage."

Helen glances over at James, her eyes hard. "I thought he was dead"

She turns back to Suzanne, the weight of those words hanging in the air.

"I hope this hurts, you Horde son of a bitch."

BANG.

Helen fires a single shot into Suzanne's head, her face exploding in a gruesome spray across the backdoor. The body collapses in a heap on the floor. Helen straightens up, walks over to James, and leans her shotgun against the wall. Her expression softens as she places a hand on his cheek. James doesn't flinch. Every instinct tells him to trust her.

"Horde?" he asks, but Helen doesn't respond, her focus shifting to her own questions.

"How are you standing here?" she whispers, almost too softly to be heard.

James is at a loss for words. Does she have the answers to his past, to why he feels such a powerful connection to her? Her touch sends warmth through him, deep into his soul.

"I thought I lost you for good. How...?"

A noise behind them breaks the moment, the warmth fading as Helen pulls her hand away. Suzanne's body is moving, her arms flailing, searching for the head that no longer exists. Helen glances at James' forearms, and both of their eyes widen. The markings on James' arms begin to glow again, but now he notices that Helen's arms bear the same markings, brighter, more intricate, with what appears to be ancient script from different cultures, glowing blue.

"If you don't know who I am, then you might not know what happens next," Helen says, her tone shifting. "This might freak you out. Stand beside me, arms outstretched. Like this."

Helen positions herself over Suzanne's body, extending her arms to her sides. Reluctantly, James mirrors her stance. A low hum vibrates through the room, and Suzanne's body struggles against an invisible force. Gravity intensifies around her, pinning her to the floor.

James feels his own arms being pulled down, held by the same force. His head suddenly fills with excruciatingly sharp pain. He tries to grab his head, but his arms feel too heavy. The strange markings on his arms have returned and burn a bright white light. He needs to get out of here.

CHAPTER 2

Energy courses through Helen's arms like two repelling magnets, and the bright markings on her forearms start to emit electric-like charges. One shoots out, striking Suzanne's foot, which explodes on impact.

Helen turns to say something, but when she looks, James is gone. The door swings shut behind him, and she realizes he's left. She doesn't chase after him, there's no point shouting over the hum of energy filling the air.

She turns her attention back to the now screaming Suzanne.

Chapter 3

The tenement block, built in Edinburgh in the late 1970s, is being prepped for demolition to make way for a new business park. A large metal fence with barbed wire surrounds the buildings. All the residents moved out several months ago, and the site is lit by generators running day and night to deter trespassers, which usually works. Work on the site has halted after asbestos was discovered in several buildings, leaving the council and the construction company squabbling over who will pay for its removal.

In a worn and dirty flat on the third floor, James has set up a temporary base of operations. The flat, stripped of furniture during the clean-up, now holds only two sleeping bags in the corner, a duffel bag full of clothes, and a police handheld communication radio. Photographs of people and buildings are pinned to the wall, some marked with red pen, including a family portrait of the Jones family.

James, a young Black man in his early twenties, sits at what was once a kitchen counter, engrossed in his laptop. A packet of crisps and a can of juice sit beside him. With earphones over his closely shaved head, he listens to loud music while his

CHAPTER 3

fingers fly across the keyboard, flicking between windows.

The door to the flat creaks open, and James, dressed in torn, dirty clothes and a filthy blanket he stole, steps inside. He glares at the back of Peter Frankford Collins, known as Pete, and approaches him silently. Crouching next to Pete's bag, James pulls out a weapon. Pete freezes mid-chew as he feels the cold end of a pistol pressed against the back of his head. He presses a key on his laptop, and the music stops. A half-eaten crisp falls from his mouth.

"Bang, you're dead," James says, removing the pistol from Pete's head and placing it next to the laptop. He takes a handful of crisps from the bag.

Pete removes his headphones and looks James up and down, noting his dishevelled appearance. "You look like crap. What happened?"

"Your intel was wrong. The name you gave me was the only one in the house who wasn't a demon, not the other way around."

Pete's expression shifts to shock as the realization sinks in. "You killed her?"

James doesn't answer. Instead, he begins changing his clothes, pulling jeans from his bag. Deciding not to pursue that line of questioning, Pete asks, "Why would they pretend to be a family but keep one human? Has this ever happened before?"

James stands up, holding a t-shirt, and walks to the bathroom door. Turning to Pete, who has just asked a question, James replies, "Horde."

Pete looks confused. "Quoi?"

"Something happened tonight, and I don't know how to explain it. She knew me. She said 'Horde,' and then there was electricity coming from her arms."

James pauses, staring into space for a moment. "Wait, what?"

He takes a swig from Pete's can, then heads into the bathroom. Pete hears the shower turn on and stands to shout at James but stops himself. He paces the room, muttering "she," "Horde," and "electricity" repeatedly.

James emerges from the bathroom, clean and refreshed, fully dressed except for socks and boots, with damp hair. He opens the fridge, grimaces at the smell, and closes it again. "What is it with me and fridges?" he asks.

"She, Horde, Electricity?" Pete repeats, ignoring the comment. He looks at James with a worried expression. "Remember Prague?"

Pete shudders and raises a hand, but James cuts him off. "Prague was not my fault, and you know it. We were given that address as a drop spot. How was I supposed to know it was a setup?"

Pete's eyes widen. "You destroyed a whole city block across

CHAPTER 3

from a school. We were lucky it was at night, or the casualty numbers would have been much higher. I'm not built for that kind of guilt, mate." His East London accent thickens with his agitation.

"Okay, maybe I got a bit carried away," James admits. "We need to speak to your contact who gave us that address. I promise, I'm just going to ask questions. I won't even take any weapons. Well, maybe a knife. Possibly a grenade."

Pete opens his mouth, but James cuts him off. "I'm kidding. Anything on 'Horde'?"

"A lot, but I don't know what I was looking for. It's a term for a large group or gang, sometimes made up of about five families. It's used in games and TV. It dates back to the 1200s with the Mongols, up to the Turks in the 1390s. What did you mean by 'she' and 'electricity'?"

James updates Pete on everything that happened at the house.

"Should we be worried that a woman who can shoot electricity from her arms knows who you are but you don't know her?"

"I didn't say she shot electricity from her arms. I don't actually know what happened. My head got too sore, and I left. She does know me and seemed surprised I was alive," James explains.

Pete frowns. "You said she mentioned the word 'Horde.' What do you think she meant?"

"I don't know. We need more intel. Set up the meeting," James says, rubbing his temple and thinking.

Pete sighs and turns his laptop around to show James a map of the city with a dot on the left-hand side. He hovers his hand over the keyboard. "Are you sure we want to do this?" he asks.

James leans in to study the screen and then stands back up. Pete, unsure how to process the information, knows that James has very little memory of who he is. He also suspects there is something more than human about him—his speed, agility, and ability to heal from almost any injury, including regrowing an arm.

James saved Pete's life when Pete's world was destroyed, making him like family. Pete also suspects James is much older than he appears but has never brought it up. Maybe now is the time to start asking questions. One question stands out.

"I think tonight is the night I go with you on a mission. What do you say?"

James tilts his head in disbelief. "Absolutely not. You aren't ready, and this isn't the time."

James stands up, holding a t-shirt, and walks to the bathroom door. Turning to Pete, who has just asked a question, he replies, "Horde."

Pete looks confused. "Quoi?"

CHAPTER 3

"Something happened tonight, and I don't know how to explain it. She knew me. She said 'Horde,' and then there was electricity coming from her arms."

James pauses, staring into space. "Wait, what?"

He takes a swig from Pete's can, then heads into the bathroom. Pete hears the shower turn on and stands to shout at James but stops himself. He paces the room, muttering "she," "Horde," and "electricity" repeatedly.

James emerges from the bathroom, clean and refreshed, fully dressed except for socks and boots, with damp hair. He opens the fridge, grimaces at the smell, and closes it again. "What is it with me and fridges?" he asks.

"She, Horde, Electricity?" Pete repeats, ignoring the comment. He looks at James with a worried expression. "Remember Prague?"

Pete shudders and raises a hand, but James cuts him off. "Prague was not my fault, and you know it. We were given that address as a drop spot. How was I supposed to know it was a setup?"

Pete's eyes widen. "You destroyed a whole city block across from a school. We were lucky it was at night, or the casualty numbers would have been much higher. I'm not built for that kind of guilt, mate." His East London accent thickens with agitation.

"Okay, maybe I got a bit carried away," James admits. "We need to speak to your contact who gave us that address. I promise, I'm just going to ask questions. I won't even take any weapons. Well, maybe a knife. Possibly a grenade."

Pete opens his mouth, but James cuts him off. "I'm kidding. Anything on 'Horde'?"

"A lot, but I don't know what I was looking for. It's a term for a large group or gang, sometimes made up of about five families. It's used in games and TV. It dates back to the 1200s with the Mongols, up to the Turks in the 1390s. What did you mean by 'she' and 'electricity'?"

James updates Pete on everything that happened at the house.

"Should we be worried that a woman who can shoot electricity from her arms knows who you are, but you don't know her?"

"I didn't say she shot electricity from her arms. I don't know what happened. My head got too sore, and I left. She does know me and seemed surprised I was alive," James explains.

Pete frowns. "You said she mentioned the word 'Horde.' What do you think she meant?"

"I don't know. We need more intel. Set up the meeting," James says, rubbing his temple and thinking.

Pete sighs and turns his laptop around to show James a map of the city with a dot on the left-hand side. He hovers his hand

CHAPTER 3

over the keyboard. "Are you sure we want to do this?" he asks.

James leans in to study the screen and then stands back up. Pete, unsure how to process the information, knows that James has very little memory of who he is. He also suspects there is something more than human about him—his speed, agility, and ability to heal from almost any injury, including regrowing an arm.

James saved Pete's life when Pete's world was destroyed, making him like family. Pete also suspects James is much older than he appears but has never brought it up. Maybe now is the time to start asking questions. One question stands out.

"I think tonight is the night I go with you on a mission. What do you say?"

James tilts his head in disbelief. "Absolutely not. You aren't ready, and this isn't the time."

"Are you kidding me? This is exactly the time. Your head is all over the place with this mystery woman who knows you, and I can see you find something familiar about her. I'm not pushing, but I'm right. I can also see you trying to hide your sore head. Is it like the others?"

"No, this one is worse but also different. There's something else that will blow your mind."

James pulls up the sleeves of his top, revealing black tattoos that resemble geometric mystical language all over both forearms. Pete jumps out of his seat, staring in complete bewilderment.

"Where the hell did they come from?"

Pete examines the tattoos closely, turning James's arms over and taking several photos with his phone.

"I just noticed them in the shower. They must have been hidden by all the dirt and blood."

"They look like a mix of ancient Aramaic, Egyptian symbols, and cutting-edge computer code, with some intricate geometric mathematics thrown in. Do they hurt?"

James watches as Pete continues his examination.

"No, but I can feel them now, like a faint current running through them. When Helen told me to stretch out my arms, I did it instinctively, like I'd done it before. There was a rush of power from my arms towards that creature. It wasn't painful, just like pins and needles times a million. Now that I think about it, Helen had similar markings on her arms."

"Wait a minute. The woman who knew you her arms had the same tattoos as you, and she did some crazy magic thing. Why didn't yours?"

"My head felt like it was going to explode, so I left. From a few houses away, it looked like a storm was raging inside the house, like a tornado or something. Then the house exploded, like a

CHAPTER 3

gas eruption, but there was no fire. I didn't see anyone come out, so I don't know if they survived. I wasn't sticking around to find out. The markings on my arms faded afterward."

"Oh, and just to be clear, you're not coming tonight. If this source of yours deliberately fed us bad intel, things could go south very quickly. Don't rush this, Pete. Your time will come. Okay?"

Pete takes a step back and slumps onto his stool. "Fine, but it better be soon."

"Good lad. Have they replied?" James asks.

Pete spins around to his laptop. A chat box is open on the dark web, and he sees a message from the user "Dont@skQ." He scribbles it on a notepad beside his laptop, rips off the paper, and hands it to James without lifting his head. He hates this part, never knowing if it's the last time he sees James. James takes the paper, gently places a hand on Pete's shoulder, then grabs a small rucksack and his jacket before leaving the flat.

Chapter 4

The room is nearly in complete darkness, except for a single line of firelight seeping through a crack in the door. The light stretches across the room, barely illuminating the wall opposite the door. The only sound is a scraping noise, like nails running up and down something made of stone.

As the door opens wider, more of the room becomes visible. The outline of a large figure sitting on a stone throne emerges. A hand with razor-sharp nails scratches at the throne's arm, suggesting the sitter is lost in deep thought. The walls and floor, now illuminated, are all made of stone.

A large, cloaked guard steps back out of the room after pushing open the meter-thick stone door. In their place, another cloaked figure enters—this one is nearly three times smaller and hunched over like someone very old.

"My apologies for the interruption, my lord," the snake-like voice hisses from the hood of the cloaked figure in a language not spoken in centuries. The figure on the throne remains motionless, showing no sign of acknowledgment.

CHAPTER 4

"They have found him. They have found the one."

The scratching claws come to a halt.

Chapter 5

"Seriously, is this how you thought coming here would go?" the raspy voice taunts.

A claw pierces through James' chest, narrowly missing his heart, pinning him to the wall across the bar. Blood drips from his pale chin and neck, soaking his t-shirt. His broken body dangles over shattered glass and scattered furniture. Behind the grinning man who holds James against the wall, snarling creatures with sharp teeth watch him with hunger. They all want a piece of him, but something is stopping them. The man pinning James to the wall must be their leader. He struggles to contain his large belly in a white t-shirt that reads "I EAT HUMANS." He is covered in cheap blue tattoos, matching his leather biker jacket and trousers, which sport the words "Order Killers" and a picture of an angel on fire. All his companions wear similar jackets. His long beard does little to conceal the sharp teeth gnawing on a lit cigar. The room resembles an English tavern from the 1800s, but with modern lighting and a jukebox, which had been playing British rock before James was thrown in.

"You Order boys are getting really sloppy with your intelligence,

CHAPTER 5

aren't you?" the biker says with a thick Manchester accent.

James coughs up more blood, struggling to breathe. He lifts his head off the wall, stretching it as far as he can toward the biker.

"What the hell is an Order boy? I just came for the atmosphere."

A skinny, weasel-faced biker lunge at James in response, but the leader's other massive arm grabs the weasel's face. He growls, crushing the weasel's face, bones crunching as muffled screams escape. The leader's hand opens, and the weasel collapses to the floor, twitching. The leader turns his gaze back to James with a smile.

"Anyone else gets too excited, and you'll get the same."

The group steps back from the leader and James but remains ready, like jackals waiting for their prey to tire.

"Where were we? Oh yes, you were trying to provoke me, so I'd throw you across the room and you'd have a chance to escape. Now that you know I'm not as stupid as my friend on the floor, let's have a chat. Like proper gentlemen."

He retracts his claws with a slurping sound but grabs James by the scruff of his neck before he hits the ground. He drags James to the other side of the room, lifts a couple of chairs, and wipes the table clean of broken glass and chair fragments with James' face. He then places James on a chair, his face cut from glass shards and smeared with beer. The leader sits opposite him, and the bikers form a circle around them. The leader looks up and says, "Get us a couple of drinks, but none of that Scottish crap. I might be in this scummy country, but I'm not drinking their piss water. Good English ale."

James picks several shards of glass from his face and uses his t-shirt to wipe away blood and drink. His right arm, still broken, is slowly healing. The wound in his chest drains all his energy, leaving his body to catch up. He flicks a shard of glass into the face of the nearest biker and laughs, but the pain makes him stop. The biker steps forward but hesitates, lowering his head in defiance to the leader. The leader takes a long draw from his cigar and blows smoke into the air.

"It's illegal to smoke in a place of business, you know," James says.

He pulls another shard from the back of his head and flicks it at the same biker. "Let's get the pleasantries out of the way before we talk business, shall we?"

Ignoring James' comment, the leader's booming laughter fills the room. "In all these centuries, why have we never crossed paths before? I've heard the stories about you. I even requested a few times to meet you, but I was always denied. We almost crossed paths by accident in 732 at the Battle of Tours, but fate intervened. The same happened at the Battle of Hastings."

James scans the other bikers, holding their gazes longer than necessary. "I have no idea what you're babbling about, but I'm sure it works on all the ladies in here. All I wanted was to meet

CHAPTER 5

a friend and have a quiet drink. You're the one who got weird."

"You know, looking at you, it's hard to imagine you're the famous slaughterer of the Horde. If I hadn't been informed by the Royal family, I wouldn't believe it myself. You certainly look like you've been through hell. Coming in here with no backup and acting like you... don't... remember..."

The leader's realization strikes him, but before he can speak, the biker James threw glass at lunges at him. The leader, moving with astonishing speed, catches the biker mid-air and throws him back. The biker crashes against the wall and hits the ground hard. Roaring, he springs onto all fours, ready to pounce. The leader, now standing, pulls out a handgun from the back of his trousers and fires several shots into the biker's face, pushing him back. The leader laughs again, places the smoking pistol on the table, and turns to the others.

"He almost impressed me, but hesitation is what separates you from me."

James glances at the nearest biker to his right, who glares at the leader with rage that isn't directed at him. "You going to take that from him?" James asks.

The leader turns to James, then to the biker, but before he can speak, the biker rushes forward. His claws stretch to several inches long, and with a single swipe, he tears off the front of the leader's face. The biker then drives all five fingers into the leader's exposed face and pushes through up to his elbow. Their combined momentum sends them crashing over a broken table. The biker lands on top of the leader, who falls heavily. The biker tears a chunk the size of a melon from the leader's neck and shoulder with his razor-sharp teeth. The leader's collarbone juts out, arterial blood spouting into the air. The leader lies motionless, and the other bikers show their satisfaction with toothy grins. The biker stands and looks at James.

"Pick him up. I don't care who you are or if you know who I am, but one thing is for sure: we're going to eat every inch of you until there's nothing left to heal from."

The biker grabs James by the throat and throws him over the bar, slamming his back against the mirror on the wall. James falls hard onto the body of a young woman. He rolls off and sees her crushed head, with her remaining eye staring at him in a look of terror. A biker grabs James by the jacket and drags him away from the bar. In the scuffle, James grabs the bright pink, bloody rucksack from the girl's shoulder. He is shoved back into the chair he was sitting in before.

The roar of the bikers is cut short when the side wall of the room explodes, sending wood and plaster flying. Several bikers close to the wall are shattered into pieces, their blood mixing with plaster and dust. Visibility drops to nearly zero as the lights go out and the shouting is muffled by the ringing in James' ears. He is on his side, not remembering falling, but the heavy biker torso on his legs suggests that might be why. Rubbing his eyes, James looks around and sees a biker across the room catching something in his hands. As realization dawns on the biker's face, the grenade explodes. James surveys the carnage; the

CHAPTER 5

bikers, now less shocked, are trying to regroup.

Through the smoke and debris, James sees Pete standing in the hole, holding a Hatsan Escort pump-action shotgun with an ammo belt slung over his jeans. Pete points the shotgun at a biker on the ground trying to stand and fires a round into his face. The biker's head explodes, and Pete pumps the grip. Another biker leaps at Pete, but Pete fires before the biker lands, sending him flying back as if pulled by an elastic band. Pete frantically fires more shots at any movement. James gets up, and Pete swings the shotgun towards him and fires. James moves to the side, but not quickly enough; a couple of shots hit his shoulder, spinning him around before he collapses to the floor. Pete drops the shotgun, which swings at his side on its strap. He rushes to James, who is clutching his blood-soaked shoulder.

"Oh Jesus, sorry man. I didn't see it was you."

"You didn't see at all, did you? What the hell are you doing here?" James groans.

"By the look of it, I should have come sooner."

"Do you have any idea what you've just walked into?" James asks.

Pete helps James to his feet and hands him a SIG Sauer P229 pistol from his hip holster. James takes it and checks the chamber with one hand. As the dust in the room begins to settle, Pete looks at the hole he made and readies his weapon.

"Of course, I know what's going on. I have you bugged," Pete says.

Before James can respond, Pete is yanked backward and thrown across the room. He lands hard, hitting his head on the floor and feeling dazed. He doesn't move immediately, feeling intense pressure on his chest. Straining to look, he sees the now fully healed leader holding him down with a boot. Across the room, James moves into a weaver stance and aims his pistol at the recovered leader. The leader rips Pete's shotgun from his body, the straps coming away like paper, and pumps the weapon, aiming it at Pete's face. He glances around the room; only a few bikers are still standing, the rest are healing on the floor.

"Looks like I missed a lot," the leader growls.

He turns to James, tilts his head, then looks down at Pete and back up at James with a slightly baffled expression. The leader's face hasn't fully healed and still has missing pieces, including his left eye.

"This child is human. You aren't here on Order business, are you?"

It's a statement rather than a question. James doesn't answer. He takes his finger off the trigger, opens his palms, and slowly lowers the pistol, tucking it into the back of his trousers. He stretches his arms out to the side.

"That is sagacious of you to surrender. We will sit down like

CHAPTER 5

before, and you WILL answer my questions," the leader says.

Suddenly, the leader's eyes widen, and he tries to raise the shotgun at James, but he's frozen in place. James's eyes are closed, and the tattoos on his arms begin to glow a bluish white. In his peripheral vision, the leader sees the other bikers are stuck in place. A wind starts to pick up in the room, pulling slightly toward James. The electricity emanating from James causes his whole body to glow white.

"James!" Pete yells.

"I can't control this. Get out the way you came in!" James strains to shout.

The wind turns into a gale, swirling around James and lifting furniture but keeping the bikers in place. Blue flames flow from James's forearms, licking the leader's skin, while bolts of electricity strike around the room.

Everything abruptly stops, as if someone has cut the power. James collapses to his knees, his head pounding as though it might explode. The symbols on his arms dim, and his muscles ache.

Pete, who had followed instructions, returns to the room, wiping dust from his face. He looks around in disbelief. The bikers, as if awakening from a trance, begin to stir and stare at James.

"What is wrong with you?" Pete asks, but before James can

respond, a grenade explodes, stunning the bikers. Pete drops the grenade launcher onto the floor and moves quickly to James.

"We need to go," Pete says.

He helps James to his feet. Now feeling stronger, James leans on Pete as they head toward the large hole. Before they disappear through it, Pete throws a makeshift bomb with a timer counting down from five seconds.

Chapter 6

James sits on the floor in the centre of the room, meditating to let his injuries heal. He wears only jeans, with his top and boots beside him. Pete, in a retro Kappa tracksuit, hunches over a laptop with earphones in, oblivious to his surroundings. Despite his own sore body and cuts that will take longer to heal than James's, he has replenished some energy through sleep and food and is now deeply focused on his work. He types furiously, pausing only to grab a handful of crisps or take a slug from his massive energy drink. With an IQ over 120, he is fully in the zone.

"What will we get for dinner?" James asks, eyes still closed.

Pete doesn't hear him due to his music blaring in his ears. James sighs, picks up a boot, and tosses it into the air. It clatters onto the table next to Pete, making him jump in fright.

"Jesus, James," Pete says, clutching his chest.

Pete pulls out his earphones and turns around.

"What was that for?"

James is nowhere to be seen. Suddenly, the front door bursts open, the mortise locks flying across the room. Pete screams and jumps to his feet. A massive man, the size of a silverback gorilla, in a black suit and tie struggles to squeeze through the door frame. His black, greasy hair is slicked back, and he has a toothpick in his mouth. Following him is a thin, very pale man in a dark suit. The strange man is bald with dark purple veins popping out and wears sunglasses.

"Relax, kid. Don't soil your pants," the pale man says with a whispering American accent.

"Who the fuck—"

Pete is thrown across the room as if struck by a steel pole. He hits the ground hard and, holding his stinging face, struggles to turn onto his side with ringing in his ears. The huge man looms over Pete, nostrils flaring as he growls.

"Please watch your language, Mr. Collins, or my friend here will slap you again."

Breathing heavily and tasting blood in his mouth, Pete spits onto the floor. He is instantly grabbed by the huge man, who lifts him, pinning him against the ceiling with powerful hands around his neck.

"That will be enough now, Tiny. Let Mr. Collins speak."

Pete hits the floor, the wind knocked out of him. A shooting pain radiates from his toes to his neck. His entire body aches.

CHAPTER 6

The large man, known as Tiny, picks Pete up and drops him onto a stool. Pete places his elbows on the table, rubbing the back of his neck. The thin man steps in front of him, across the table.

"My name is Smith. This is Tiny," the man says.

Pete's brain is still catching up, unable to process the irony.

"If you tell us why you and your friend were at my establishment tonight, Tiny will squash your head quickly. The pain will be minimal."

Pete's fear is evident despite his efforts to stay calm.

"Listen, okay, I don't know what you're talking about. I wasn't anywhere." His voice trembles.

"Do not play games with me," Smith says, his tone growing cold. "I know you and your friend were at my bar tonight and caused quite a commotion. If I have to repeat myself, Tiny will rip pieces from you very slowly. Starting with your left foot."

Pete starts to laugh uncontrollably, unable to stop himself.

"Sorry, I don't mean to laugh, but do you practice talking like that, or is it natural?"

He knows he is going to die. Oddly, fear is giving way to excitement.

"Such disrespect," Smith says, glancing at his long, sharp nails. "Rip off the entire leg, Tiny."

Pete's laughter dies abruptly, his face shifting from amusement to anger.

"You two are really going to regret coming here," Pete says, his voice hardening.

He starts to prepare himself for a fight. From behind Smith, James's voice cuts through the tension.

"I was going to deal with you one at a time by making noises to draw you out, but you threatened my friend, who had a rough night. That really pissed me off."

James stands at the flat's door, now wearing his t-shirt and one boot. Tiny turns toward him, and James levels a Remington 887, one of the world's most powerful shotguns, at him. Smith straightens up, keeping his hands in view, and slowly lifts his arms, recognizing James.

"Wait—" he starts.

The loud boom of the shotgun fills the room. Tiny's head explodes like a watermelon, sending fragments of skull, brain, and blood flying everywhere. His large body collapses to the floor, twitching. James turns the weapon toward Smith, who almost grins in response.

"Sorry, you were about to say something?" James asks.

CHAPTER 6

Smith stares into James's eyes, a sinister smile curling on his lips. "I'm a bit confused. If you were at my bar, why did you leave without finishing off my bikers?"

He continues, "I've heard the stories, but seeing them with my own eyes is something else. You have no idea what you are, do you?"

Smith's face contorts into a horrific grin as he locks eyes with James, who tightens his grip on the shotgun.

"Are you kidding me with this?" a new voice interjects.

Smith turns toward the voice. James keeps his gaze fixed on Smith, his finger squeezing the trigger slowly. Pete looks from James to Smith, then to Tiny's headless body, and finally to the woman who has just appeared out of thin air.

"I haven't heard from you in almost a century, and now it's twice a week. And again, you seem to be in a really bad situation."

James tries to ignore her, still focusing on Smith. Tiny's headless body has stopped twitching and is now just bleeding on the floor.

"Listen, I have no idea who you are, how you keep finding me, or how you managed to walk away from that house, but can you just be quiet for a second?"

"This is pathetic and not something I want to be a part of. A truly rubbish reunion. You must be—" Smith starts but is cut off by both James and Helen shouting.

"SHUT UP."

Smith falls silent. Helen raises her hand toward James and waves it up and down slowly.

"James, lower the shotgun."

James doesn't move.

"James, listen to me."

Helen's voice carries a warm, familiar feeling. James hesitates, recognizing her voice. He keeps his eyes locked on Smith, whose gaze shifts between James and Helen. Pete, stunned and trembling, watches the tension between James and the woman at the door. He has seen James recover from almost anything but never understood what he truly is. The charged atmosphere between James and Helen overwhelms him.

"James!" Helen shouts.

James whips around, his anger flaring. Seizing the opportunity, Smith shoves James aside. James crashes into the opposite wall but manages to catch his balance before hitting the floor. He looks up just in time to see Smith sprint to the window and leap through it.

"Dammit, do you have any idea what you've done?" James

CHAPTER 6

shouts.

He places the shotgun on the floor, grabs his other boot, and dashes past Helen and out the door. Helen turns to Pete, who has fallen off the stool and is now sitting on the floor, taking deep breaths and starting to shake uncontrollably.

"Hi, I'm Pete," he says, teeth chattering.

Helen pauses, surprised. She picks up a jacket from the floor and drapes it over Pete's shoulders.

"Hi Pete, I'm Helen. This will stop the shivering. And drink that liquid sugar you have."

Helen takes a deep breath, leans back slightly, and then runs to the window Smith jumped through, leaping out after him. Pete collapses back onto the floor, staring at the grimy ceiling.

"I can almost hear you tutting from here, Mum," he mutters, then begins to laugh, only to stop when Tiny's nearly decapitated body starts to move, struggling to stand. Pete grabs his laptop and go-bag and rushes out of the flat.

James bounds down the steps, taking them two at a time, slowing only to pull on his other boot. He bursts through the door frame and into the close, spotting Smith clearing the metal fence surrounding the construction site without a second glance. Helen, her broken ankles and femur healing, is between James and the fence. He runs past her, ignoring her shouts.

Smith heads toward a shopping centre complex, now closing with bars, restaurants, and a large cinema. He reaches the edge of the parking lot and slows to a walk, trying to blend in. Drunk patrons leave the complex, their cars honking as they sing and shout. Smith smiles at a couple getting out of their car and approaches them, shoulders hunched.

"Excuse me, do you know what time the last bus is?"

They stop to answer his question. The man looks at his watch, while the woman retrieves her bag from the car and comes around the front. Smith grabs the man's jacket and yanks him from the car. As he lands on the ground, Smith stomps on his head, crushing it. The woman screams, but her cry is cut short when Smith reaches her in an instant. He rips out her larynx, causing her to choke, and lets her fall to the ground.

Smith gets into the car, but before he can close the door, bright lights behind him fill the rear-view mirror. The car crashes into the rear, throwing Smith's face into the steering wheel. The rear seats and bonnet crumple against his back.

James peels his face from the airbag and unclips his seatbelt. People look over and begin to approach him. A young couple starts to run but slips on the crushed skull of a man, screaming in realization. James grabs a jacket from the passenger seat and gets out of the car, limping to the front. All attention has shifted from the crash to the murdered man and woman near the car. He searches through the wreckage, but Smith is gone. James's phone vibrates in his pocket.

CHAPTER 6

"You, okay?" Pete asks.

"We need to pack up. I lost Smith, but he can't be far. I'll get you at the backup site as soon as I can."

"I've already left. Tiny looked like he was starting to get up, and I wasn't sticking around for that."

James spots Smith through the cars, heading down the ramp to the lower level of the parking lot before turning a corner.

"I see him. Stick to the plan and remember to destroy everything. Be careful," James says, closing the flip phone before Pete can respond and shoving it into his pocket. This night is getting worse.

James slowly walks down the ramp and sees that the shutters, which were down, are now bent halfway up at the corner. He crouches and slips through. The parking lot is nearly empty, with no more than five cars belonging to patrons who have decided to take a taxi home from the pub. The overhead lights are off, leaving only the illumination from four fire escapes. His eyes are adjusting to the darkness, but he knows he is at a disadvantage. James puts his hand inside the large coat he finds and pulls out nothing. It's not his coat, and he left in such a rush after Smith. Without a weapon or torch, James cautiously walks along the middle of the parking lot, past large pillars.

A car alarm suddenly goes off to his right. James turns toward it, then spins around, expecting Smith to strike from behind.

With no sign of Smith, he relaxes and resumes walking. He is kicked in the back with such force that a couple of ribs break, and he is thrown onto his front. Smith follows, jumping and landing hard with both feet on James's back. Pain erupts through his spine, and his lower half goes numb. James screams before blood fills his mouth. Smith slowly steps off his back and laughs to himself. James tries to claw at the ground and escape, but his body is dead weight. Smith walks around to his head, taking his time.

"Ouch," Smith mocks.

He rubs his head with long, pale fingers and crouches beside James. With a sharp nail, he presses it between James's shoulder blades. James gasps. Smith places nails from his other hand on James's chin, turning his face toward him. A monstrous grin stretches across Smith's face.

"You have no idea who you're dealing with. Running around, hunting 'monsters' without really knowing why. Healing from any injury—fascinating, what an immortal body can do. The High Council will be very interested in how you survived. I might even be elevated to a higher status. A Marquette, perhaps. As for your precious Order, this will really shake them up."

James tries to focus on Smith, but the pain is overwhelming.

"But before we worry about the who's and the whys, I'm going to eat your face slowly. Very, very slowly."

CHAPTER 6

Smith opens his mouth wide, his teeth stretching like a Venus fly trap. He catches a shadow in the corner of his eye and turns his head, keeping his mouth open.

"Eat this."

Helen squeezes the trigger of the shotgun, blasting the top of Smith's head and causing him to fall back onto James. Helen grabs the top of his open skull, lifts him, and throws him to the side. She bends down to James, placing a hand on his head.

"It's me. Don't move."

She stands up and pumps the shotgun, but she's too late. A staggering, almost headless Smith is making his way to the fire escape, stumbling all the while. She fires a shot, but with the distance he has gained, only a few pellets strike his right shoulder. He falls against the wall and gropes for the door. Helen starts to chase him but stops to look at James. Ignoring Smith, who has now pushed open the fire escape door, setting off the alarm, she lifts James over her shoulder and heads for the same exit, kicking it open.

"Who the hell are you and how do you know me?"

James struggles to stand, but with strength returning to his legs, he can put more weight on them.

"First, we need to get out of here. Then we can talk," she says.

He takes a deep breath and turns to her.

"I have a place not far."

His voice trails off as unconsciousness takes over.

Chapter 7

Helen surveys the room, the overpowering smell of sewage nearly unbearable. The old maintenance room features a storage area and a small office off to the side. One wall is lined with lockers, most of which are empty, though a few are open with high-visibility jackets inside. An ancient, torn sofa sits against the opposite wall, while the remaining wall displays torn posters of topless women and a large, dirty whiteboard. The only modern items in the room are a small fridge and a large black storage box with two silver clips.

James lies on the couch, covered with a blanket. He suddenly wakes, sits up, and wiggles his toes under the cover, realizing he has been unconscious for some time. He looks over at Helen, trying to recall how he got here. Pete sits on an office chair next to the couch, his laptop open with several windows running code.

"How are you feeling?" Helen asks.

"How did we get here?"

"I brought you here. Thankfully, your phone wasn't smashed,

and you had just one number on it. Your friend picked us up and brought us here."

"You really don't know who I am?" Helen asks, struggling to contain her emotions. "I've been searching for you for years. I tried not to lose hope, but there was no sign of you. I genuinely thought they had killed you, that they had found a way to kill us. I'm so sorry I gave up. I stopped looking for you."

A heavy silence fills the room.

"Why didn't you come back to the Order? Why didn't you come back to me?" A tear runs down her cheek. James takes a deep breath before responding.

"I'm sorry, but I don't know who you are. I don't even know who I am. About 25 years ago, I woke up naked with no memory. All I had was a British passport and about £200 in mixed notes."

Another silence.

"I know there's something strange about me. I can heal from almost any injury, and I've been injured a lot. I also have this weird urge or pull that's hard to explain. This pull always leads me to humans disguised as monsters, which I have to kill or put down, and that's difficult."

Helen takes a slow breath. "Those 'monsters' are called the Horde."

CHAPTER 7

Pete looks at James, who remains focused on Helen.

"We're not entirely sure where they came from, but they were here before us."

"When you say 'us,' do you mean people?" Pete asks tentatively.

Helen ignores this and continues. "Some believe they were attached to the rock that wiped out the dinosaurs, but it's just a theory. Every demon, monster, or scary story throughout history is linked to the Horde. We know they're trapped; we've been told this first-hand. The only way out is to consume and destroy the entire planet, suggesting this was not their intended destination. They've come very close to escaping a few times."

Helen walks over to the small fridge, retrieves a bottle of water, and takes a long, slow drink before putting it down.

"How long?" James asks.

Helen hesitates, unsure what he's asking but preparing herself.

"How long have you been fighting them?"

She almost lets out a relieved breath. "Before I get into that, tell me: how long have you been fighting them?"

This question throws James, who thought Helen knew him. "You tell me," he replies.

Helen raises her hands to show she's not attacking. "I mean, how long can you remember fighting them? When does your memory stop?"

James relaxes slightly but remains on edge. "I can remember the last ninety years. I woke up in a hospital in Berlin with just a British passport and some money. I travelled through Germany for about a year, checking with the police in every region to see if I was reported missing. I spoke the language, so I assumed I was from there. I didn't encounter my first demon or Horde until I was on an underground tour in Bremen. It was a late-night tour, and I was bored, so I went. There weren't many of us, but a young woman kept looking at me. It clearly bothered her boyfriend, who eventually picked a fight with me. The girl then ripped his head off and tossed it aside like it was nothing. She killed the others and attacked me. Her whole body changed into something that looked like a wingless gargoyle."

Helen hands him the bottle of water, which he accepts and drinks from. "We must have fought for about an hour before something inside me clicked. Before that, my fighting had been mostly defensive. After she threw me through a wall, she said she'd always wanted to kill me. A switch flipped, and I attacked her. I tore her apart and crushed her head until nothing was left. I ran away thinking it was just a headache from the fight, but I needed to get out. From then on, I've followed the pull to places where Horde are present. It took a lot to get used to. I've been killing these things across Europe, which led me to the UK, where I've been for a while. I met Pete a few years ago, and that's my story."

CHAPTER 7

"I hate to say this, but from what you've said, you haven't been killing them. Your sudden departure from the house shows you don't really know how to stop them. If you think you've been killing them and then leaving, they've probably just healed, maybe taken new bodies, and escaped. I'm sorry."

James swears under his breath. Helen walks over, takes his hand, and examines the black geometric tattoo on his forearm. James is startled and unsure how to react. He gazes into her eyes, then quickly shakes himself when he realizes what she's doing. Helen pulls up her sleeves to show her arms. James notices her smooth skin speckled with freckles. Why does this woman he's just met feel so familiar?

"Your tattoos should have faded by now, and they feel colder than the rest of your arm," Helen says, pondering. "Maybe it's a result of not cleansing your prey."

"The tattoos only appeared the other night, after meeting you in the house. Before that, my arms were bare."

"Curiouser and curiouser," Helen mutters to herself, turning his arms over before realizing what she's doing and dropping them suddenly.

James ignores the tattoos for now. "Who are we to each other? Why do I feel a similar pull towards you as I do those Horde things, but instead of a cold, foreboding feeling, it's warm?"

Helen is caught off guard. "I don't know what to tell you, James. You shouldn't be like this. Our kind heals from anything and has never experienced brain damage."

She takes a breath, making a decision. "Simply put, we are everything to each other. Where you end, I begin. Our suns rise together, and our hearts beat as one. That 'pull' you feel is a love we've had for over 20,000 years."

A loud electronic ping interrupts the silence. Pete turns to his laptop, tapping the touchpad. Radio chatter fills the room, and Pete begins typing rapidly. He looks up at James. "It's them."

James is still absorbed by Helen's revelation. "James!" Pete shouts, pulling him out of his reverie.

"It's them," Pete motions to the computer, shaking James.

"Get your stuff, Pete, and get to the van. Remember, two blocks away. I'll call when I get there." James stands, turning away from Helen to the large black storage case in the corner of the room. He unclips the latches and opens the lid. Inside are two CZ Scorpion Evo 3 S1 carbine automatic rifles and three Glock 17L Combat Master pistols. James takes out holsters and secures them to his belt. He then removes two handguns, holsters them, and straps the carbine around his shoulder.

"What's going on?" Helen asks.

Pete looks at her, startled, then at James, who is still preparing his gear. "I'm not getting involved," Pete says to Helen, walking to a small electronic box in the corner. He turns a key on top, and red numbers start counting down from ten

CHAPTER 7

minutes. He stuffs his laptop into his rucksack and runs out of the room, his footsteps echoing upstairs.

Helen's eyes are fixed on James, who takes a deep breath. "We've been tracking a group that hits high-end art galleries. We keep missing them, sometimes by minutes, but tonight we might catch them in the act. I don't know how, but I sense a monster or Horde is with them, and the pull towards it is stronger than anything I've felt before—more than the pull towards you."

"Art thieves?" Helen asks.

James stops and turns to her. "We've been following this group for a while. They have expensive tastes and operate like an '80s action movie, leaving a trail of death. Those who are captured never reveal the leader, almost as if they worship him. This is the first time I might get the jump on them."

"Wait, how do you know it's the same group? The police in this country don't usually provide that kind of information on the radio," Helen questions.

"It's a long story, but I'm one hundred percent certain it's them. I knew they couldn't resist it."

"Wait, you need to give me more than that. Resist what?" Helen asks.

James glances at his watch and takes a deep breath. Seeing Helen's reaction, he realizes she's not pleased. He softens, understanding that she holds answers to questions he's had for years, and he needs her.

"Along with the passport and money, I also had a slip with an address for a secure storage unit and a passcode. The items I found there were unbelievable and expensive. I've been using them to fund my operations. Since this group targets antiques, specifically paintings, I featured one in a gallery."

Helen puts her face in her hands. "Wait a minute. When you say 'secure storage,' please tell me you don't mean the one in Harrow?"

A smile crosses James's face as he realizes she knows the location. However, this smile fades when he sees the anger in her eyes. "That was my stuff, James. Are you telling me you've been using my collections to fund all this?" She gestures around the dingy room. "And you mentioned a painting. Which one?"

"Petit Pierrot aux Fleurs."

A noise erupts from Helen's gut, a mix of anger and frustration. "No, James, please tell me you didn't. He painted that for you. You know how much I love that painting. To use it as bait for some gang of art thieves—" Her voice trails off, her disappointment palpable.

"I don't remember much, but this group might be the key to discovering who I am. I need to find them; this is my chance. His name has been echoing in my mind for as long as I can

CHAPTER 7

remember, like a taunt."

He pauses, then says the name.

"Astaroth."

Helen walks to the large case, retrieves a spare carbine and three magazines, and remains silent. James senses the gravity of the name and knows it's more significant than he realized. They both leave as Pete's timer reaches ten seconds.

Chapter 8

The building was once a world-famous rug-making factory but has since been converted into a mix of office spaces and a renowned art gallery. The gallery occupies the ground, first, and second floors, while the remaining two floors are office spaces, one of which is vacant. The roof has been transformed into an artistic spiritual garden, though it's overgrown and underused due to the Scottish weather.

The entire gallery is covered in windows, which can be electrified to turn white, protecting the artwork from the sun. All the windows are activated to prevent the large group of police officers surrounding the building from seeing inside.

The gang, dressed in black tactical clothing, is armed with carbine assault rifles, sidearms, and knives. They are strategically positioned on each floor, including the roof. Each corner has a guard, and a fifth guard moves between the corners. They wear balaclava-style masks with tactical goggles and throat mics. They are fully prepared for any situation.

"Roof Five clear," a corner guard says into his mic.

CHAPTER 8

The blade in James's hand slides smoothly and silently from the back of the guard's head through his face. Letting go of the hilt, James catches the dead guard as he collapses. As the body hits the ground, James slides the knife out.

"Okay, that gives us five minutes of mic time, but the fifth man might walk over," Helen says.

"Watch his movements; he's the fifth man on the roof for a reason."

Helen observes the guard moving from one corner to the other. He has a slight limp and stops halfway to look out at the streets, rubbing his thigh.

"He has an injury. Good catch. I'll be back in a minute."

She returns moments later with the guard over her shoulder. James removes the goggles and balaclava from the dead woman and begins to take off her throat mic. Helen grabs his hand and holds it still.

"Wait. I thought it was odd that they're using expensive equipment but only standard throat mics. Look at the back of the neck—the small box isn't the battery."

Helen turns the woman's head to reveal a box with a wire running from it down her body armour to a semi-large pouch on her belt.

"Son of a..." James mutters, rubbing his stubbly chin.

"They're all rigged, with a lot of..." Helen doesn't finish the sentence but makes an exploding gesture with her hands.

James feels a sense of familiarity working with Helen, even though he has only just met her. They move and operate seamlessly, which feels right to him.

"She's Russian military, but the guy with the limp looks Middle Eastern. They don't usually mix, even as hired guns. They're not Horde, but I do sense one in the building. It doesn't make sense," Helen says.

"I'd say money crosses all borders, but the booby traps suggest otherwise. You seem to know Astaroth. Who are they?" James asks.

Helen ignores the question. "We need to be cautious with the explosives. We'll take it one level at a time and avoid setting off any traps."

James looks at Helen, but she doesn't return his gaze. "Listen, maybe—"

She cuts him off. "We have to move before anyone notices."

James doesn't press further and puts a finger to his ear. "Pete, what's your take on the wiring of these explosives?"

From a van a few blocks away, Pete responds through the earphones. "There are no signals coming from them, so I can't deactivate them from here."

CHAPTER 8

Helen eventually turns to James. "Maybe they're controlled from inside or only if they're shot?"

"Pete, I need you to contact the police and pretend to be someone still hiding in the building. Tell them you've heard something about explosives, make it convincing, and emphasize that there are a lot."

"Already doing it," Pete responds.

Helen watches James as Pete acknowledges the request.

"You two make a good team. How do you want to do this?"

"Just like you said: we take it one level at a time and avoid setting off the explosives."

"I'll take her radio; we might need it," Helen says.

Outside the building, the police begin moving their vehicles and officers back, relocating to a block away while maintaining constant surveillance. Inside, the leader of the group smiles, clearly impressed.

It takes no more than three minutes and no shots fired to clear the roof. James and Helen move and work together seamlessly, communicating without words. James uses metallic Billy Clubs and is more brutal, while Helen moves like a dancer, relying on her hands.

They reach the door leading to the lower floors. James quietly opens it, and both descend the stairs to the next door. Helen holds up an earpiece attached to one of the radios taken from a guard.

"I'll re-con the floor and come back," James says.

"Yes, because that always goes well. Or have you forgotten that time in Persia?" Helen stops herself, realizing her slip. She's getting too comfortable and forgetting this isn't the James she remembers. James tries to brush off her comment. He opens the door before Helen can stop him and walks through.

"Wait here," James says, emotionless.

Helen lets the door close and bangs her head against the wall. "Dammit."

BANG. BANG.

Muffled shouting and more gunfire come through the door. Helen hears a guard through the radio.

"This is Four-One. There's someone in here with us. He's taken out Seven and Three. We need—" The voice cuts off.

More gunfire and shouting follow, then the stairwell door opens. Helen is greeted by a beaten and bloody James.

"Yeah, yeah, I know," he says, rubbing his shoulder.

"No explosions?"

CHAPTER 8

"That's the weird part. They didn't have explosive collars on. What the hell is going on here?"

"Come on, we don't have time to figure it out. More could be on their way after that last broadcast," Helen suggests.

Helen steps onto the fourth floor, surveying the damage and carnage from James's re-con. She draws her carbine from under her coat, checks the chamber, then looks at James before pulling the radio from her pocket.

"James, is that you?" a gravelly Russian voice asks over the radio.

James moves closer to Helen. "Is that him?" he whispers.

Helen lowers the radio, her hand shaking. She feels out of place.

"Pete, our cover's been blown, and shots have been fired. Have the police noticed?"

There's no response from Pete. James looks at Helen.

"Your friend can't hear you now. It's just the three of us. Yes, Helen, I know you're with him, so no need to be shy."

The Russian voice now comes through both the stolen radio and the ones James and Helen are wearing. James moves his hand to his ear, but Helen shakes her head and throws the stolen radio away.

They storm through the floors, tearing apart anyone who stands in their way, ignoring who has or hasn't got an explosive collar. The entire third floor detonates, shaking the building and shattering windows across the street. They reach the stairs just as flames engulf the building. The explosion draws the attention of the police and the media, who have now arrived.

Helen and James pause on the stairs leading to the second floor to tend to James's injuries. He was the last one through the door and has fresh burns on his left arm, shoulder, and the left side of his face. Helen retrieves bandages from a conveniently placed first aid kit outside the second-floor door, sits him down, and wraps his worst burns.

"You okay?"

"I used to be faster. Must be old age," James winces with a laugh.

Helen continues to bandage his shoulder. He will heal, but the pain remains.

Suddenly, the door to the second floor bursts open, and a towering, muscular white man in dark clothing enters the stairwell. He has a large scar that runs from the top of his bald head, through his left eye, and extends just below his chin in a straight line. The mountain of a man wraps his massive hands around Helen's face and head, lifts her off the ground, and throws her through the open door.

"Boss is tired of waiting on you," the man says with a Russian accent.

The Russian man moves toward James, who is struggling to his feet. James raises his hands into a fighting stance but then changes his posture, palms open toward the giant man.

"Wait," James shouts in Russian.

The Russian man halts his advance, and James notices he isn't wearing an explosive collar.

"I'm not in any condition to fight right now. Why don't I just walk with you wherever you want me to go? Can I pick up Helen on the way?" James asks.

The Russian man laughs.

James's head feels like it has been crushed in a vice and then run over by a truck as he slowly opens his eyes. He wonders if he'd still have both arms if he'd fought the Russian. He sits up and sees Helen lying on the floor next to him. Sliding over to her, he gently touches her shoulder. She jolts and raises a fist.

"Easy, it's me. You okay?"

"What ran me over?" she asks, her voice strained.

Helen puts her head in her hands as James helps her into a sitting position. Her left shoulder is drooping. She looks at it, then at him. He holds her arm and with a sharp motion pops it back into place. She lets out a sharp, short breath through clenched teeth.

"Ouch, that looked excruciating. But man, did you handle yourself like a warrior."

James snaps his head around toward the low, gravelly Russian voice. Astaroth stands across the room, dressed in the same tactical clothing as the others. With his cropped military-style hair and clean-shaven face, he stares at them with black eyes and a creepy grin.

Astaroth walks over, takes an assault rifle from the nearest guard, and examines it.

"CZ Scorpion Evo 3 S1 Carbine with a modified suppressor. Very nice, very nice indeed," Astaroth says, admiring the weapon.

He points the rifle at one of his men and pulls the trigger. With a spurting sound, three rounds fire into the guard's chest, throwing him to the floor.

"Getting a hold of one must have been arduous and certainly not cheap," Astaroth remarks.

James tries not to meet Helen's gaze. Astaroth looks at the weapon with an impressed expression and, without much effort, snaps it in half.

"I almost forgot to ask, Helen my dear, how is young Miles?"

Helen doesn't react. Astaroth walks over to them with a big

CHAPTER 8

smile, showing his shark-like teeth.

"No response?"

He waves his hand dismissively.

"Ignore me. I'm in a funny mood. I wasn't expecting to see you tonight, my dear. Anyway, it's been a long time, Helen, and you're looking as radiant as ever. It is Helen now, isn't it?"

She doesn't answer.

"The look of complete disdain and anger really brings out the colour in your eyes, don't you think, James?"

Astaroth says this to the large Russian man, who lets out a single laugh. Helen's body tenses, but she waits for an opening. Astaroth then turns to his armed men.

"These two have been together since the beginning, and when I say beginning, I mean THE beginning. They are the original power couple, although that changed some time ago, I believe."

He laughs.

"Nice touch with getting the police to move further back outside, but I'm afraid that's what gave you away. You always get overexcited and sloppy, James. Helen, though, I'm very surprised. You were always the level-headed one. I'll chalk it up to being apart for so long."

Astaroth walks around them, admiring them as though they are works of art.

"Oh yes, I'm up to speed with all your recent goings-on, James. Lost and thought dead. Forced to wander the lands with no memory of who you are, with an unknown pull toward the evils of the night. Killing your way across Europe. Blah, blah. Sounds like a 1920s movie reel. Very dramatic."

He places his hand on his chin, as if pondering.

"We've been watching your fumbling with great delight, James, but this has been a surprise encounter. You've travelled across Europe on your little crusade with no clue what you were doing. Then, as if the gods intervened, Helen finds you. Romantic, if you think about it."

Astaroth stands, looking at the two on the ground.

"Tell me, is that your real accent or have you watched too many '80s movies?" James asks, showing no emotion.

"Please, James, show some respect. If you're going to address me at all, use my title," Astaroth says, waving his hand grandly.

"What?"

"Oh yes, you only know my name from the intel we've been feeding young Peter," Astaroth comments, a flash of something dark crossing his eyes.

CHAPTER 8

Before James can react to the mention of Pete's name, he feels a surge of dread. He has always been careful to protect the kid.

"Allow me to introduce myself again, James. I am The Great Duke Astaroth, 64th demonic spirit of the Ars Goetia. Commander of the 36th Legion and destroyer of the only true thing you and your beloved Helen ever truly loved. Solomon gave us such dramatic titles, did he not?"

Astaroth bows.

"Poor Anna. She was dreadful for my digestive system; I was picking her intestines out of my teeth for days." He smiles.

Helen leaps to her feet, charging at Astaroth in a fit of rage. With no effort, Astaroth grabs her by the throat and slams her to the ground. He kicks her in the stomach with such force that she slides back to where she started. James looks around the room at the guns aimed at them. Whoever Anna is, there's a history here. Is this the reason for James's unknown obsession with Astaroth?

Astaroth waves his hand dismissively, and his men lower their weapons.

"What were we saying? Ah yes, you don't like the accent, Tovarich?" Astaroth chuckles.

They remain silent.

"I like to change things every few years to keep them fresh. I enjoy the sound of this accent; it's powerful, very Communist, full of mystery. I think it's quite fitting these days, don't you?" Astaroth says.

James keeps his gaze fixed on Astaroth while keeping an eye on his men. He feels Helen doing the same.

"I shall, however, revert to the last voice you would have heard from me: The King's English," he says in a perfect English aristocratic accent.

"Oh, and thank you for setting this trap for me. The Picasso was an excellent touch, but you failed to see, through your foggy memory, that it was I who was setting a trap for you. Even with no memory, you're so predictable."

Astaroth pauses, watching them.

"I have one question. If this was a trap, why bother sending your men to get me at the flat first?" James asks.

"Say again?" Astaroth stops.

"The thin, unhealthy-looking one and his friend who looks a lot like your Russian guard there. Why go to all that trouble to send them for me when you seem so confident I would come after you?" James nods toward the giant Russian.

James takes a step forward.

"I have no idea who you are or who this 'Anna' is you claim to

CHAPTER 8

have eaten—gross, by the way. You seem confident, with your accents and your bowing, showing off how strong and big you are. Do you know how expensive that weapon was?"

It takes Helen a few seconds to realize what James is doing. Even with no memory, he still knows how to be a pain. She can see Astaroth shifting his stance, tightening his jaw, trying to hide his anger.

"You claim to know about my memory loss but still go to all this trouble to draw me in. Doesn't that seem a bit much? What was it you called yourself?" James takes another step forward. "Great Duke? Come on. You aren't that great if you went to all this trouble, and as far as villain monologues go, yours was pretty pathetic. 'Great Duke'? Pfft."

Helen almost smiles.

The smile vanishes from Astaroth's face, replaced by a low growl. James seizes the moment and charges at Astaroth, but this time more slowly. He is intercepted by two guards, which was the plan. With everyone's attention on James, Helen cracks the nose of the closest guard with her elbow and grabs a pistol from his side holster. With precise shots to the head, she drops three guards before anyone can react, two of whom had their hands on James. She then fires three more shots into the giant Russian—two in the chest and one in the head. This is James's cue. He charges forward, using his momentum to take down the flanking guards with ease. The pain from the explosion has faded.

Astaroth takes several steps back as more of his men storm the floor through the doors. The smile returns to his face and grows wider as he watches James and Helen fight, taking down their opponents—Helen with gunfire and James with his bare hands. Astaroth hates humans, but no more than he hates the two in front of him. They took away his chance for a higher title and humiliated him in the Court. In return, he took everything from them.

Astaroth examines his manicured nails with boredom as he crosses the room. He picks up one of his dead guards' rifles and points it at the fight. With a squeeze of the trigger, he fires. Everyone collapses—except one guard. James and Helen lie on the floor with bullet holes in their torsos and several limbs.

Astaroth removes his tactical vest and belt, then his protective suit. Underneath, he wears a dark navy two-button suit, a white shirt, and a dark purple bow tie. He glances at his watch, then at James, crouching beside him.

"I wish I had more time to find out who visited you earlier, but as the rabbit says, I'm late."

He stands, winks at James, and fires a single shot into his head. The bullet shatters the back of James's skull, sending blood spraying onto Helen's face. Astaroth then fires a single shot into Helen's abdomen, shattering her spine. He discards the weapon and stands over the surviving guard, who raises his gun weakly, blood filling his mouth. The guard tries to speak but struggles.

CHAPTER 8

"Go on, child. Free yourself," Astaroth says to him.

The guard doesn't wait for another offer. He fires, but death comes too quickly, and he only manages to hit Astaroth in the shoulder. The shot causes Astaroth to stumble dramatically. He screams and wails around the room.

"Ah, the pain, the pain. How can I endure this agony?"

He stops screaming, straightens up, and regains his composure.

"Not the shot I had hoped for, but I must adapt to situations. Now, you two don't go anywhere. My audience awaits." His accent shifts to the East Coast of Scotland.

Astaroth walks over to the giant Russian, who lies motionless on the floor. He rummages through the Russian's pockets and makes a positive noise. He pulls out a remote and presses a few buttons, glancing at James and Helen.

"Tick tock."

Astaroth clears his throat, then runs to the stairs. As he descends, he begins to scream in terror. He bursts out the front door, crying and shouting.

"Help me, please! I've been shot. They shouted something about going with a bang before I could escape. Help me, please!"

Helen tries to move but is immobilized by her injuries. She feels the searing heat of the fires as the room erupts in an explosion around them.

Chapter 9

Pete strolls down the corridor, doing his best to blend in. Dressed in blue overalls and a work belt, with overhead headphones on but no music playing, he nods his head to an imaginary beat and makes occasional vocal sounds. Chewing gum and clutching a clipboard, he projects an aura of "I work here but don't want anyone talking to me."

At three in the morning, this part of the hospital is mostly quiet, with only the occasional porter passing through. The corridors, mostly lined with storage rooms and the occasional box or bed, are deserted. Pete knows that no one wants to engage in conversation or make eye contact at this hour, fearing additional tasks. He is aware that this path leads to the mortuary but had to take a detour due to construction blocking the direct route.

He lets out a sigh of relief as he turns a corner and spots the double doors leading to the mortuary. Removing his rucksack, he examines the security sensor, which requires a card for entry. It should be easy to bypass, just like the one he dealt with earlier.

Crouching down, Pete opens his large backpack to retrieve the adapter. He notices the door on the left and almost laughs.

"So much for keeping the dead secure."

He slips his backpack back on, pushes open the unsecured door, and lets it close behind him. Taking out his flash light, he scans the dark, quiet corridor. After a careful walk, he reaches a T-junction. Turning left, he stops. The corridor has rooms on either side, each with clipboards hanging on the wall. Inside each room are nine freezers. At the end of the corridor is a desk for staff. Pete enters the first room on the left and shines the light on the clipboard. He quickly scans the names, then moves to the first door on the right and repeats his search. He stops at numbers eleven and thirteen, both marked with UNKNOWN.

Pete enters room thirteen and turns on the fluorescent light. The bright light reflects off the white tiled walls and floor, taking a moment for his eyes to adjust. He approaches freezer thirteen, opens the door, and slides out the long tray. The tag on the body bag reads UNKNOWN and POLICE, with a date. Pete unzips the bag from head to feet, revealing a naked James.

"Morning, sunshine," Pete says, setting down his rucksack.

James's eyes slowly blink open, and his right hand moves to the spot where he was shot in the head.

"What time is it?"

James sits up and sees Pete unpacking clothes from his bag.

CHAPTER 9

"Just after three. Are you okay?"

Pete hands James clothes and trainers.

"Yeah. I got shot in the head and think I only regained consciousness recently. What about Helen?"

Pete walks over to door number eleven and knocks.

"She's in here."

James watches as Pete jumps with fright when the door knocks back. Pete opens the door and pulls out the tray, then turns his back to it.

"What are you doing?" James asks, finishing putting on his trainers.

"She'll be naked, and I don't want to embarrass her."

"Her or you?"

The body bag Helen is in shifts, and her annoyed voice comes through.

"Can you get me out of this thing, if you two aren't too busy?"

Helen finishes dressing and joins James and Pete outside the room. She approaches Pete, who is shining his flash light up the corridor, and places a hand on his shoulder.

"Nice job on the clothes sizes, by the way."

Pete blushes and stumbles over his words, trying to respond. Clearing his throat, he leads them up the corridor. Helen tucks the Glock into her jeans, concealing it with her t-shirt.

"This way to the exit. There shouldn't be anyone here, so we can—"

Before he can finish, all the corridor lights switch on. James grabs Pete's arm and pulls him into the room across from where they came. They back into the corner of the room and wait.

Around the corner come two identical twin sisters in similar overalls to Pete's. Their long black hair is tied back in tight buns, and one of them holds a tablet. Both have ID badges: one reads Black, and the other reads Peterson.

"It's this one," Black says with a strong Boston accent, pointing to the room on the right.

"Are you sure?" Peterson asks.

Black holds up the tablet, making a face.

"I was just asking. No need to be a bitch."

Peterson snaps back, "I was just asking for clarification. You didn't need to make me feel stupid."

CHAPTER 9

Black puts her hands on her hips. "I'm not being a bitch. You just asked a stupid question."

"I was just asking for clarification, and you didn't need to make me feel stupid," Peterson insists.

"Can we just get on with this? This place gives me the willies."

BANG

"You two were taking too long," Helen says, as the gunfire echoes through the corridors. The hole in the wall near Black's head doesn't faze her or James. They stand in the corridor, pistols aimed at the sisters, who turn to each other, smile, and then face Helen and James.

"Are you two supposed to be scary?" Black asks.

"Be nice. They did save us some work," Peterson adds.

The sisters laugh, which slightly confuses Helen.

"Who are you?" Helen asks.

"Horde?" James asks, looking at Helen.

The sisters laugh even louder. Helen fires at the wall again, causing them to laugh a bit less.

"These two aren't Horde. They're too stupid," Helen comments.

The sisters stop laughing. James stands ready, anticipating they might rush them.

"We aren't stupid. We found you, didn't we? That was our plan," Black says smugly.

Black throws the tablet at James, who fails to react in time and gets hit in the face. James fires a shot into the ceiling before Black leaps at him, knocking him to the ground.

Helen reacts quickly, firing two rounds into Peterson's right shoulder, then delivering a punch to the wound. Peterson screams, drawing Black's attention.

"You bitch!" Black shouts.

The distraction gives James an opening. He grabs Black by the bun and smashes her face into the wall until her body goes limp. James pushes her off him and stands up just as Helen throws Peterson to the ground.

Peterson glances at her sister with concern. Helen nods, allowing Peterson to go to Black. Pete peeks his head out of the room now that things have quieted down.

"Let's try this again," Helen says, standing over the sisters. Peterson, the only one conscious, looks at Helen.

"Who are you, and how did you know we were here?"

Pete approaches James, who is nursing a scratched face.

CHAPTER 9

"How did you know they weren't real hospital workers?"

"Their name badges were different. If they were real workers, their names would match," James explains.

Pete considers this, then adds, "What if one or both were married?"

James doesn't have time to respond as Helen walks over.

"We need to go. There might be more coming."

"What did she say?"

"Nothing helpful. Let's go," Helen replies.

They leave the sisters where they are and make their way through the hospital to Pete's van in the loading bay.

Chapter 10

She feels the rain on her face, mingling with her blood and pouring into her swollen eye. Her long brown hair is soaked with rain and blood. She would wipe the blood from her face if her hands weren't bound above her head to the stone altar she lies on. Her ankles are bound too. The pain she feels now isn't from the large gouge in her head caused by oversized razor-sharp teeth, but from the thirty-centimetre deep clawed laceration across her stomach. She has survived worse injuries in her long life, but this time there's a sense of finality. She tries to keep her breathing steady. She has had many names throughout history, some known for her talent as an architect. For now, she is known as Patricia.

"Do you know what makes a good story?"

The croaky, bodiless voice comes from behind her. She doesn't recognize it, but she knows who it is, sending a shiver through her. Confusion and fear overtake her, and her breathing falters.

"Origin. Everyone likes, no, loves, a good origin story."

The voice moves closer. His hands land gently on her shoulders,

CHAPTER 10

and she jumps.

"About two hundred and fifty million years ago, stop me if you know this, a large rock travelled through the solar system and crashed into its third planet. This caused intense volcanic activity in what we now call Serbia. Huge volcanoes, acidic rain—literal hell on Earth."

His large, taloned hand runs up her bare arm. She cannot stop shaking.

"Sorry, that's my origin story and not yours."

She feels his face on her left cheek as he moves beside her. His breath is warm, almost burning.

"I get so confused sometimes."

He removes his hand from her shoulders, and she clamps her eyes shut, feeling him move around her slowly.

"Do not close your eyes. I have not told my story yet."

His croaky voice is strong. She doesn't open her eyes; she can't. Her body shakes uncontrollably, fear overwhelming her.

"OPEN YOUR EYES OR I WILL RIP THE SKIN FROM YOUR FACE AND FEED IT TO YOU."

Her eyes snap open. The large shadowy face is inches from hers. It moves back and stands in front of her, folding his arms. She is outside but hears nothing, indicating she is somewhere remote. The rain falls on her, and she hears a distant thunderclap.

"It is 30,000 BC," the voice begins.

She jumps at the voice now behind her again.

"Tell me if you have heard this before I go on—actually, don't. I don't like being interrupted when telling a good story."

He pauses, and she remains silent. He nods, almost thanking her for complying. He walks around her, his steps heavy.

"In 30,000 BC, or thereabouts, in what is now France, lived a tribe of one of the earliest forms of man—or, if I were to sound scholarly, a tribe of Cro-Magnon."

His hand thrusts inside her stomach, pulling out her intestines. He turns them over in his hand before pushing them back inside her. The wound slowly heals itself.

"Typically, in those days, males hunted, females bore children and made meals. They roamed the land, grunted at each other. However, on a cold and clear night, something spectacular happened to this tribe."

His hand swipes across her throat, slicing it open. She spits out blood and gargles, struggling to catch her breath.

"A fireball flew across the sky and crashed several miles from

CHAPTER 10

where the tribe was grunting."

She lets out a shout as her larynx heals, her breathing causing her pain.

"Anyway, this tribe of grunters decided to travel to where the fireball landed."

She screams in pain as ten talons stab into her legs, pulling out chunks of muscle.

"The tribe eventually arrived at their destination, but instead of finding a fireball, they found a dull rock. You see, the fireball crashed into a mountain, exposing a system of caves. Inside one cave was a black, crystal-like rock. It was big, about twice their height. Nothing special apart from its appearance, but with lava rocks all over the region, it was nothing to behold. What most scholars and historians don't know is that this tribe had what would be known as a warrior caste, or dedicated hunters depending on who you ask. This was made up of both men and women of the strongest and bravest who protected the tribe."

A long talon swiftly removes her ear, and another talon digs into her right eye, pulling it from the socket.

"The warriors approach the rock while the others set up a makeshift camp. As the warriors get closer, they realize this is no ordinary rock. It emits intense heat yet feels cool to the touch, and there's something... unnatural about it."

The figure's large fists slam down onto her torso with a thud. Bone crushes beneath them, and blood explodes from her mouth. She whimpers from the excruciating pain.

"The leader of the tribe, a large and strong warrior, signals for the others to wait while he enters the cave to explore. When he gets inside, he realizes he is not alone. They aren't the only ones drawn to the fireball's landing site. Another creature arrived before them and is moving around behind the rock, hidden in the shadows. The leader sees the creature and approaches it."

The talons slice across her face in a single swing.

"The other warriors wait anxiously for their leader to return. The scream from the cave is unmistakable—a short, guttural cry. All the warriors rush to the cave's edge as their leader emerges, walking slowly."

He pauses.

"My apologies; I was lost in a memory. Where was I? Ah, yes."

The talons dig into her healing torso.

"The leader, with his back to his warriors, turns to face them and smiles. His mouth curls into a grin, revealing more and more teeth. His eyes, once human, are now as black as the rock. The warriors stand in shock at the sight of the monster that used to be their leader. The battle is fierce and bloody. Before they can subdue the rabid, snarling creature, it leaps over their

CHAPTER 10

heads and attacks the entire tribe—old and young, no one is spared. The beast laughs with a mouthful of children. You can still hear the crunching, can't you?"

She hears something heavy being placed on the floor and footsteps walking away, indicating someone else is present. The sound of clasps unlocking a box fills the air. A strange chill spreads across her skin, like a freezer opening or an ice-cold waterfall rushing over her.

He goes silent again, this time for longer. Patricia's thoughts turn to escape. She needs to survive this and warn the others.

"Listen. We can fix this. You don't have to do anything you'll regret," she says, her voice trembling. Her body is still broken and torn, but her vital organs have healed, and other wounds are being treated.

Her voice falters, replaced by a bubbling gurgle. Blood spurts from the deep slash across her throat. She tries to remain calm, knowing the wound will heal, but something feels wrong. The wound is frozen, the same cold she felt when the box opened spreading through her. Patricia tries to turn her head and sees him walking back, wiping blood from a long, curved blade. He turns to her, his large, sharp teeth forming a smile.

"Sorry, you were saying?"

He walks toward Patricia, holding the knife out so she can see.

"Do you like it?"

He moves the knife around, showing it to her from different angles. Patricia tries to speak, but only a gargle emerges. The wound on her throat should have closed by now; her windpipe should have healed enough for her to breathe.

"That's right, child. You are going to die."

Patricia tries to escape, panic now replaced by survival instinct. She struggles to pull her hands free to grab her throat but fails. Her body starts to convulse from lack of oxygen.

"I want you to know before you die that I will wipe out the rest of your kind, one by one."

Everything begins to blur as darkness creeps into the edge of her vision.

"My Lord, there has been a problem," says another voice, deep and echoing as if from the bottom of a dark well.

Patricia feels the blade pierce her heart before she realizes it is being thrust into her chest. Her entire body feels as though it's caught in an ice storm. The knife is pulled out and wiped on her shoulder.

The rain continues to fall, and thunder roars overhead.

The woman now known as Patricia Gilliard is dead.

Chapter 11

Pete drives through the streets, sticking to the speed limit and stopping at every red light. James sits in the passenger seat with Helen in the middle. Helen has just finished giving them a brief history of the Horde and an organization called the Order of Solomon.

"So, you and this Order, who have the backing of every government, travel around the world hunting creatures that look like demons but can also look human. You're telling me they're responsible for all the worst things throughout history?" Pete asks.

James remains silent.

"I know this is hard to believe," Helen begins.

"You have just said you and James are some kind of super humans who can't die and heal from anything?"

"We're not super, and there are things that can slow us down or incapacitate us, but yes, we cannot die. As I said, this might seem overwhelming."

Pete lifts his hand off the steering wheel to interrupt Helen.

"This actually answers a lot of questions I've had. To be honest, there's a lot on the dark web about what you've just told me. I dismissed it as conspiracy theories. You guys should be concerned about security leaks."

Helen laughs and puts a hand on Pete's. Human contact isn't something Pete is used to.

"Who do you think is putting all this information online? We've found that leaking information is a great way to make it seem unbelievable. Most people would rather believe it's made up by paranoid communities than accept the truth. We've been doing this a long time."

Helen turns to James.

"Do you have anything you want to ask? You've been very quiet."

"I don't think he's finished," James replies, pointing at Pete.

Helen turns back to Pete but then looks past him out the window. Her gaze moves forward.

"I know where we are. I should have been paying more attention. Pete, turn left at the next traffic light and then stop next to the post box."

Without asking any questions, Pete follows her instructions.

CHAPTER 11

James shifts in his seat, sitting upright. Pete stops at an old post box on the pavement beside the road.

"Let me out," Helen asks James.

He follows her around the van to the post box. Pete rolls his window down and hangs out of the van. Helen slips her hand into the letter slot and clicks something on the roof of the box. The sign on the front, which displays the postal service badge and pickup times, pops open. She opens the door to reveal a black, clunky communication device attached to a charging cable. She takes it and closes the door.

James follows her back into the van, but Pete remains in place. Helen looks at both of them and answers their unspoken questions.

"The Order has drop boxes all over for emergencies or if we need to grab new clothes, like this."

She lets that sink in before continuing.

"I don't want to take you back to the Order yet. We need more information about what's going on, and you didn't leave us on the best terms."

"Best terms? What the hell does that mean?" James asks, slightly annoyed. He's been wondering for decades if the Order has something to do with his memory loss.

"You have to trust me, James. We'll go to the Order soon, but I need more time. There's something going on here, and I want to understand it before it's taken out of our hands."

Helen turns on the SAT radio. It crackles for a few moments, then emits a low tone followed by a monotone voice from the small speaker.

"Connection established. Voice verification required."

"Alpha two, Code seven five three," Helen says into the mic after pressing the button to talk.

"Verification complete."

The speaker clicks a few times before a new voice comes through. This time, it's a young male voice.

"This is Control. We have your location. Do you require extraction?"

Helen motions for them to relax.

"Copy Control. Negative on extraction. Put me to work."

"Understood. Standby."

The controller provides Helen with an address. Before they can ask her anything else, she turns off the radio and throws it out Pete's window.

They can still track it, and once word gets out that it's me

CHAPTER 11

asking, they'll track us. Pete, drive, and I'll direct you. The controller gave Helen a code after the address.

"So what does the code mean?" James asks.

"The easiest way to describe it is a Horde nest. Some Horde can create soldiers from humans. You fought some of them at that house. It doesn't always work out the way they want, so they discard them. Once discarded, they stay in one place, hidden—almost like mindless drones addicted to drugs. They are completely harmless. We've tried to help them, to save them, but we've failed every time."

"You said 'almost mindless'," James notes.

"They have a bit of a pecking order. Sometimes, the leader can give information on local Horde activity. Sometimes. But with our limited resources, it's all we have. You in?"

"Why not," James replies.

Helen directs Pete several blocks before he parks at the side of the road, across from a row of flats with various shops below them. The area is rundown, almost empty except for early risers heading to work.

"Pete, you stay here. No arguments," James instructs.

"Stay in the car or go into those flats? Yeah, I don't think I'll argue," Pete replies.

James gets out of the van and opens the side door.

"We won't need any weapons. They won't attack us."

James gives her a side glance and reaches into the van. He pulls out a 12-gauge double-barrelled shotgun, stuffs a box of cartridges into a rucksack, and throws it over his shoulder. He slides the door closed and runs after Helen, who is already across the road.

"You won't need that."

"The last time I didn't think I needed something, it took me a week to grow back my arm, leg, and liver. I'd rather have something and not need it than not have anything and, well—"

"Lose an arm, leg, and liver?" Helen finishes.

James walks to the metal door of the flats, situated between two shops, and points at it. The metal door is intended to keep people out and was fitted by the city council. The padlock has been forced open and never reported to the council.

"When we get in here, you might see some things that are disturbing. Don't make any loud noises or sudden movements. They get scared easily, and whatever you do, don't try to save anyone. There's no point, and it'll just make you feel bad."

James follows her in, and the smell hits him.

Inside the block are six flats, two on each floor. Their entrances

CHAPTER 11

are at either side of the close, with a stairwell in the centre. The stairwell has lighting, but due to the dirt covering everything, it is poorly lit. There is no rubbish, but there are signs of human and animal excrement everywhere. The doors to every flat have been either forced open or removed entirely. What little furniture remains is either outside the flats or destroyed within. Due to the smell, no one goes into the block; it is almost condemned.

Inside the flats are about forty occupants. Curtains or black bin bags taped to the glass cover the windows. The carpets are worn away, and the walls are dirty and bashed in. Their clothes are almost rags from wear and tear, and their skin hasn't seen sunlight in years. Throughout the flats, they huddle in small groups, crouched with their heads almost touching the bare wooden flooring. Several bodies lie around, having been eaten by others when they become too hungry. For now, they are almost resting, unaware of their surroundings. That changes when James and Helen cross the threshold of the block. At once, they open their eyes, their pupils dilate, and their mouths salivate as their stomachs growl.

Chapter 12

James walks down the ground floor corridor, a nauseous feeling washing over him. Helen turns and sees him leaning against the wall, rubbing his eyes.

"They're here. The feeling you're having is a twisted version of the pull we experience with the Horde. It will pass, but it's unpleasant, and you won't get used to it," Helen explains.

"What do you call them?" James asks.

"Mimics."

James steadies himself and smiles at Helen, who smiles back. He decides to change the subject.

"You mentioned earlier that we can heal from almost any injury. What's the 'almost'?"

Helen tilts her head, listening, then straightens up.

"We can regrow limbs and organs. The only thing we can't regrow is our head. If it's severed or destroyed, it heals or

CHAPTER 12

regrows independently from the body. We need to reattach the head or place it back on the body to reconnect."

As Helen speaks, they walk through the ground floor flats, finding them empty. They begin descending to the first floor.

"That sounds—"

"Yeah, it feels exactly how it sounds."

"Has there ever been a time it wasn't reattached?"

Before Helen can answer, she raises her hand, silencing James. She points upward and then to her ear.

A low hissing sound drifts from the stairwell, coming from many mouths.

"Is that them?" James asks.

Helen draws her pistols, readying them. Without thinking, James readies his shotgun.

"I thought you said these things were harmless?"

"They are. But I've never heard them hiss before. Something's wrong."

They walk into the flat on the left, where the door has been forced open, though the lights still work. They move cautiously down the hallway, peering into empty rooms, all stripped bare of furniture, carpet, or wallpaper.

"That feeling you're getting means this flat isn't empty."

James doesn't reply but feels the truth of it. He's on the verge of vomiting.

They enter the living room, with a kitchenette on the left. In the centre, three men crouch on the floor, facing each other. Their clothes are ragged, and they gnaw on a shared arm, teeth chattering. The stench of rotting flesh overwhelms the room.

"What now?" James asks.

"We need to find the alpha. Only they respond to our commands—"

Helen doesn't finish. All three Mimics turn toward them in unison. Their skeletal faces are twisted, animalistic, snarling and hissing as the sound echoes from upstairs.

"I'll ask again—what now?" James whispers.

What happens next nearly knocks Helen off her feet.

"Order should not have come," the three Mimics hiss in unison, their voices reverberating through the building.

"Don't hold back!" Helen shouts, firing three rounds into the Mimics' heads. The bullets push them back but don't drop them. They almost seem to smile. James grabs Helen's arm,

CHAPTER 12

pulling her back just as the Mimics leap toward her. He shoves her behind him, raising his shotgun. One shot obliterates the closest Mimic's knee; another shot drops a second Mimic. Both fall, hissing—not in pain, but unable to stand. James strikes the third Mimic with the butt of the shotgun, forcing it back, before reloading and firing as it charges.

Without pausing, they rush out of the flat and head for the stairs. Behind them, a stampede of Mimics races down, clawing at one another to reach them.

"Don't stop!" James shouts.

Helen skips steps, barely staying ahead. James feels the Mimics closing in, snapping at his heels. They burst from the building, shouting toward Pete, who sits half-asleep in the van. Startled, Pete struggles to start the engine.

Pete leans out the window to ask what's happening but freezes when he sees the swarm of Mimics spilling from the doorway. They trip over one another, some falling in the street, desperate to catch James and Helen. Pete opens the van's side door just in time for James to jump in and pull Helen after him. He slams the door shut as a loud thud shakes the van—Mimics are already on it.

In a panic, Pete fumbles to get the van in gear. The Mimics, now surrounding the van, bang and scratch at the windows, doors, and panels. Their nails and knuckles split with the force, but they feel no pain. Though not particularly strong, their sheer numbers make the glass begin to crack.

"What the hell are these things?" Pete screams.

James grabs Pete by the shoulders, lifting him into the passenger seat. Helen slides over to the driver's seat and immediately starts the engine.

"I need an opening," she calls back to James.

James pulls two cartridges from his rucksack, loads the shotgun, and places his foot on the side door handle.

"Ready?"

Helen revs the engine, keeping the clutch in.

"Go!" she yells.

James pushes the door open with his foot. Five Mimics lunge toward the van. James fires, obliterating the faces of two Mimics and pushing them back. The others scramble over the bodies, trying to get in. James reloads and fires again, clearing the way.

The gunfire draws the other Mimics' attention, and Helen floors the accelerator, knocking down two more in front of the van.

They don't get far before a Mimic launches through the driver's window, crashing into Helen. It bites and thrashes on top of her as she struggles to keep control, her foot still on the gas. The van veers onto the pavement, crashing into a shop next to

CHAPTER 12

the flats they had just fled.

Helen fires six rounds into the Mimic, which slumps on top of her. James pulls it off, then turns to check on Pete.

"You okay?"

Pete jumps at James' touch, nodding shakily.

"What did we hit?" James asks.

"Where we started," Helen says, staring out the cracked wind shield.

"You have got to be—" James begins, but he's cut off by the sound of banging and scratching from the back of the van. He jams the shotgun into the door lock to keep the Mimics out and then joins Helen and Pete, who are staring into a six-foot hole in the shop's floor, leading to what appears to be a basement.

"Oh no, this isn't good," Helen says.

"What the hell is that?" James asks, walking around the hole to the opposite side. He notices an open door leading toward the flats. They must have missed it while escaping.

"These Mimics weren't abandoned here. They've been placed here for a reason. The Horde uses tunnels to connect their networks, to remain unseen. They've done this for centuries. They used to connect them to large trees, scaring locals into thinking they were witches or warlocks. But why they'd link a

Mimic nest to one is new to me."

"Honestly, I think you're making half of this up. We're not under a tree. Actually, where's the closest park?" James wonders aloud.

"James, focus! This hole shouldn't be here, and I don't know why the Mimics are acting this way or how they have access to Horde tunnels."

James looks at her. "Do you think we were meant to find this?"

"I don't know," Helen says. "But I'm starting to think I was meant to find you."

A long silence lingers until Pete walks to the van.

"Those things stopped trying to get through," he says.

James and Helen turn toward the van just as a faint, distant sound echoes from the hole. James squints.

"Was that a gunshot?"

Chapter 13

Pete runs his hands along the tunnel walls, feeling the grit and cold stone. The six-foot-wide tube poses no issue for him or Helen, but James has to crouch slightly to fit. The tunnel offers just enough dim light for them to navigate without tripping, and it smells of freshly turned soil, as if it had just been dug. They descend gradually.

After what feels like miles, the tunnel begins to brighten, but it also narrows. By the time it opens into a large, warehouse-sized room, the three of them are crawling on their hands and knees. James is the last to squeeze out, landing on a smooth concrete surface. The room is about twelve meters square, lit by several bright ceiling lights, and entirely made of concrete. Wooden crates fill much of the space, but something else immediately catches Helen's attention.

"This is definitely not Wonderland," Pete mutters to himself.

James stands, dusting off his hands, and pats Pete on the shoulder before heading over to Helen. Before he can ask what's wrong, she moves to a corner of the room and crouches over three black military flak jackets. Beneath them, she finds three SA80A2 rifles.

"These are Order weapons," Helen says.

"How do you know?" James asks.

Helen looks at him but doesn't respond. He takes the hint and drops the question. James then wanders around the room, occasionally feeling the crates as if trying to open them, but without success. On one wall, he notices a pair of double doors, large enough for a forklift to pass through. After making a circuit of the room, James returns to Helen, who is still inspecting the rifles. Pete sits nearby, his back to the wall, typing on his laptop.

"What have you got?" James asks.

Pete closes the laptop, stows it back in his bag, and looks up, his face weary. "I can't get a signal on my phone, and there's no Wi-Fi down here. I have no idea where we are."

"What is this place, Helen?" James asks.

Helen stands up, handing James one of the rifles, which he easily accepts. "At a guess, it's a storeroom."

Before James can comment on her obvious answer, she cuts him off. "I'm not being sarcastic. I know what this is, but I don't know where this is. None of this makes sense. Let's find out where that gunshot came from. But stay alert—can you feel it?"

CHAPTER 13

"Horde," James replies.

"And more Mimics," Helen adds.

James tightens the straps on Pete's flak jacket, then checks his own, making sure their magazines are secure in their pockets. His rifle is strapped to his body, and he nods to Helen, who is waiting by the door.

"I have no idea what's on the other side or what the layout is. Pete, stay behind James, and if shooting starts, find cover," Helen instructs.

Pete gives a thumbs-up but instantly regrets it. Just as Helen opens the left-hand door, a voice from the other side makes her freeze.

"Don't move!"

Helen glances at James and shrugs. Before he can react, the voice, with a Cajun accent, continues with a laugh. "I'm sorry, I couldn't resist."

Helen steps out of the room, followed by James, while Pete hesitates but peeks out, instantly regretting it.

The next room is the same size but lacks the crates. In the centre, to Pete's shock, is a red leather chaise longe resting on a Persian rug that nearly covers the entire floor. Illuminated by a wooden lamp, a very fat, sweaty man lounges on the seat in a white suit with a black shirt. Two Mimics, resembling guard dogs with their torn clothes and pale skin, pace beside him. At the foot of the chaise longe sits a young girl with long blonde hair, dressed in a matching white suit. Her eyes are closed, and she mutters to herself.

Behind the man, a large spotlight beams across the room, leaving most of the space in shadow, allowing James and Helen to remain hidden.

"Where's the smart retort, or even an expletive?" the fat man shouts, his voice filled with mockery.

Pete follows the light and spots two men, and a woman pinned to the opposite wall with metal rebar through their shoulders. Though clearly in pain, they try to mask it, much to the fat man's amusement.

"You three were much more talkative before you got pinned to the wall. Not so clever now, are you?"

"Shut the hell up!" the woman pinned to the wall yells, squinting against the harsh light. Her outburst triggers a loud laugh from the fat man, shaking his entire body. He pulls a silver Magnum .44 from beside him and fires at the wall, narrowly missing her head. Pete, realizing the danger, quietly retreats and returns to the tunnel.

The man, now frustrated, closes one eye, sticks out his tongue, and fires again, this time hitting the woman in the stomach. She screams in pain, but the girl at his feet remains unresponsive. "That's better," he coos. "Now tell me, how did you find

CHAPTER 13

this place, and did you manage to report back before Berith caught you?"

Berith doesn't wait for an answer. He fires the remaining rounds, hitting the two men and the woman again, their screams furling his twisted laughter.

From the shadows, James and Helen watch silently, though Helen's eyes flick to the Mimics, uncertain if they can sense her presence. Usually, she'd be sure, but these Mimics seem different. She fails to notice James leaving the shadow, anger building in him as he steps forward.

"Hey, fat man! Why don't you point that thing at someone else? Or better yet, drop it and grab a snack," James calls out, walking into the light with his rifle still on his back.

Berith, caught off guard, stares at James in shock. The Mimics immediately lunge at him, but with swift precision, James pulls his rifle and shoots them both mid-air. They drop dead at his feet. He then fires another round into Berith's hand, sending the Magnum flying behind him. Berith lets out a scream, his mouth widening grotesquely, his teeth retracting into his gums.

The three prisoners stare at James, stunned by his boldness. James straightens up. "I think it's time to let these people off your torture wall, don't you?"

Berith, recovering from the shock, grins. "Oh my, what a treat, just like he promised. So beautiful," he muses.

"James, look out!" the woman pinned to the wall shouts.

Before James can register how she knows his name, Berith bellows, "Take him!"

A flood of Mimics pours from a door behind Berith, rushing past him toward James. As the prisoners struggle to free themselves, James opens fire on the oncoming horde. Amidst the chaos, Berith laughs, but it's cut short when his head suddenly explodes.

The Mimics freeze mid-charge. James, confused, turns to see Helen emerging from the shadows, her rifle smoking.

"You have to kill the source. These Mimics won't stay down for long," Helen says.

"He's a Horde?" James asks, already guessing the answer.

Helen doesn't respond, her attention shifting to the prisoners, who have collapsed to the floor, bloody but alive.

Suddenly, the young girl on the chaise longe lets out a high-pitched scream, her eyes wide open. The sound is unbearable, causing everyone to cover their ears. As the scream fades, Berith's head begins to regenerate. Now enraged, he leaps at James with shocking speed, throwing him across the room with a powerful tackle. In one swift motion, he strikes Helen, snapping her neck.

The battle intensifies as the others struggle to hold Berith

CHAPTER 13

down. Helen, miraculously still alive, gets back on her feet, her body glowing with energy as she and the woman from the wall prepare to finish Berith off.

James, now on the edge of consciousness, watches helplessly as the wind increases, before the darkness overtakes him.

Chapter 14

James feels the restraints on his wrists, ankles, and across his chest. He tries to take in his surroundings before opening his eyes. An announcement over the intercom requests a doctor to pick up the phone line. He's in a hospital, and the intravenous line in his left forearm indicates he has been placed in a medically induced coma. This explains the groggy and fuzzy feeling in his head and the dry mouth. The bullet hole in his head has fully healed, suggesting he has been away from the gallery for a long time and probably raised a lot of questions.

The floor outside the room is eerily quiet, which isn't a good sign. There's something else: he's not alone, but he can't hear any breathing. This can only mean one thing.

"I know you're awake," a voice says.

James opens his eyes, adjusting to the fluorescent light. At the end of his bed stands a uniformed police officer, who smiles.

"Hey, Jimmy, you look like crap. I see you're doing as well as always. How long has it been?" The officer has a strong Bronx accent, but his uniform isn't from New York. The hospital

CHAPTER 14

doesn't feel American either.

James tries to shift for comfort, forgetting about the restraints. He doesn't recognize the officer but feels the cold sensation he gets near demons. His veins seem to freeze.

"I need to tell you that killing me is going to be a lot harder than you think, monster. Why don't you take off these binds, and we can make it a fair fight?" James growls.

Valac stands up and walks to the side of the bed, picking up a cup of water with a straw and placing it in front of James' face.

"You'll pop a vein if you don't calm down. You might not remember this, but we go way back, and trust me when I say we're old friends. You've been out for a while, so your mouth is as dry as a nun's. Well, you know." He smiles.

James stares at the officer, then strains his neck. After a few attempts with the straw, he manages to take a drink.

"Small sips, Jimmy. You were out for a while."

He sips slowly.

"Who are you, and what do you want?"

James takes another sip before Valac yanks the cup away and puts it down.

"You're an arsehole, you know that? You have no idea how

much work it's been to keep you out of a deep, untraceable hole. If I were here to hurt you, you'd be a smear on these walls."

Valac walks to the end of the bed, shaking his head.

"The name's Valac. Despite being enemies since the dawn of time, you and I have become mutual acquaintances. We've helped each other over the years, and I'm here to aid you this time."

"Why should I believe you?" James says, trying to slowly free himself from the bindings.

"You're like a child sometimes; I can see your arms moving. Does this answer your question?"

In a swift motion, Valac slashes at the bindings with razor-sharp claws. They fall to the ground, without touching James.

"Now, before you try to jump up and attack me, remember you've been pumped full of drugs, so you'll be light-headed at the very least."

He's right. James slowly lifts his heavy head. Deciding to follow his instincts, he sits up on the bed rather than attacking.

"I came to check on you, especially with all the memory loss. You've been keeping yourself busy, which has kept me busy keeping you off the radar. The incident at the house was a step too far, though, and that got you a lot of attention. However,

CHAPTER 14

what you uncovered last night might have worked in your favour. The Kings aren't happy with what Astaroth has been doing, and I've been sent to collect him."

"Wait a minute," James manages, his head spinning.

"He has a lot to answer for and has been hiding from the Council. What you did last night was significant for us. You don't have to worry about Astaroth anymore. I need to know you understand what I'm saying, and you need to make Helen understand too."

"What do you mean about the house being a step too far? What was in that house?" James demands.

Valac is at James' side in an instant, claws around his throat. His face, filled with rage, is close to James's, with teeth extending into points and eyes black as glass.

"I may be in your debt, but do not treat me with disrespect. Forget the house and tell me you will forget about Astaroth. Make sure your mate understands too," Valac roars, spitting on James's face.

"Can I have another drink?" James struggles to say.

Valac relaxes his grip and steps back. His appearance slowly shifts to resemble a human as he picks up the cup. He drinks the water through the straw, then drops the cup onto the bed.

"You need to put this to bed, Jimmy. Both of you. Forget the house and return to hunting low-level Legions."

James stares at Valac.

"So why are you here—in this room?"

A ping from the lift makes Valac glance over his shoulder. He tips his police hat and nods before walking to the door.

"Oh, and ask for a deep brain stimulation; that might help things. Once you get that, consider my debt paid. Get it before Tabula Rasa," Valac says.

Before James can ask anything further, Valac is gone. James drops his head onto the pillow.

He lifts his head again when he hears footsteps approaching. Four people are walking down the corridor towards his room. He hears a pair of dress shoes with a limp and a quieter tap, possibly from a cane or walking stick, a woman in heeled stilettos, and two sets of military-style boots.

The door opens, and a 78-year-old man with white, groomed hair and a neatly trimmed beard enters. He wears a navy tailored three-piece suit and brown brogue shoes and carries a wooden cane with a twisted brass knob. He doesn't look pleased.

The woman standing beside him has cropped, slicked-back black hair and wears a black trouser suit with a white shirt. Although she doesn't look as unhappy as the older man, she's

CHAPTER 14

still not thrilled to be there. Her right eye is slightly grey, not matching its green twin, and she carries a large rucksack. James recognises her as the woman who was with the two men.

The two men standing guard wear similar suits to Samantha but are much larger, making their jackets look like they might burst if they move.

The elderly man taps the floor with his cane three times and introduces himself.

"I am Miles Fotheringham, and this is Samantha. I know you don't know us, but we know who you are, James. We're here to bring you home and would appreciate skipping the explanations for now. We don't have much time."

Miles leaves the room, followed by the two large men. Samantha smiles at James.

"You are such a dick," she muses, her accent matching James'.

"What?" James replies, completely confused.

Samantha throws the rucksack onto the bed at his feet and sits in the corner chair. James sits up, his head no longer pounding, and opens the bag to reveal a retro multi-coloured 80s shell suit. James looks up at Samantha, who is grinning from ear to ear.

"Don't forget the footwear," she adds.

James pulls out a bright blue pair of Crocs. Samantha laughs heartily as he puts them on. She stands up and gives him a big hug.

"How are you, little brother?" she asks, squeezing him tightly.

"I don't know who you are," James says, feeling overwhelmed.

She lets go, and he sees tears in her eyes.

"You called me little brother. Are we family?" he asks, nervously.

Samantha holds his shoulder.

"In the Order, we're all family, but us, James—we're really family. I thought you were gone," she says tearfully.

Without thinking, James pulls her close for another hug.

"I don't know how, but I believe you. I just wish I could remember you," he says, releasing her.

"When Helen reported back that she found you, we came straight away. Miles will want a full debrief, so save your story for that. I'm just glad you're here."

"I take it that Miles isn't happy with me?" James asks.

Samantha pauses.

CHAPTER 14

"You've been away for a long time, James. I know you have no memory of us, but a lot has happened with the Order. It's been stressful for all of us, especially for Miles. Your being alive and with no memory has shaken us all."

"What you found at that house confirms our suspicions."

"Again with the house? Valac mentioned the same thing. What was so special about it?"

Samantha turns to walk to the door but stops when she hears James's comment.

"Did you say Valac?"

"Yes, he was in the room just before you arrived. He mentioned that the two of us have a history," James replies.

Samantha puts her finger to her ear. "Valac was just here. Search the area. I didn't sense him, but he's known to avoid detection, so be cautious. He may have a connection with James, but he despises the rest of us," she instructs through her radio and waits for an acknowledgment.

"Saying you two have a connection isn't a lie. I never liked it, but he has helped you over the years, always to his own benefit. I've never been fond of your arrangements, especially because he hates the Order and has proven it several times. You can include what he said in the debrief. Let's go."

She looks James up and down and smiles.

The service lift opens into the service bay at the rear of the hospital. James and Samantha exit and walk to the black government-looking vehicles waiting for them. Samantha nods toward one of the cars and gets into the other. James opens the rear passenger door to find Helen inside. She smiles at him warmly, as if welcoming a child into a new world. He closes the door and walks around to the other side.

They travel for about ten minutes through moderate traffic and into the City Centre of Glasgow. They navigate one-way streets, with both vehicles staying close and every traffic light turning green for them. They turn and stop outside the main entrance to Central Station. After several angry beeps from black Hackney taxis, the drivers of each vehicle exit and pause for a moment. The rear door of the first car opens, and Miles Fotheringham painfully exits, cursing the high seats of the car, followed by Samantha. Helen and James follow them as they all make their way into the station.

Chapter 15

Opened in 1879, Glasgow Central Station is one of the largest and busiest train stations in Scotland, with trains departing to destinations across the country and beyond. Thousands of passengers pass through daily, whether for business or tourism, many drawn by its beautiful architecture. This bustling hub was chosen as the location for the United Kingdom headquarters of the Order of Solomon, established here after the old train station was destroyed in the early 1900s.

As they enter, James immediately spots the plain clothes security personnel of The Order mingling with the crowd of travellers and commuters. He almost laughs at the absurdity of it all—the idea of a secret organization's base hidden beneath a busy train station. Despite the tension in the group, James knows this is just a show. He has a vague sense of familiarity with the place and is aware of multiple secret entrances to the base below, but they're entering through the most public one.

He follows Miles and Samantha closely, with Helen bringing up the rear. She hasn't spoken to or acknowledged him since he got into the car, but he can tell she's nervous. They head toward the public toilets on the left and descend the stairs. As they reach the bottom, Helen leans in close to James, catching him off guard with her scent and proximity.

"You okay?" she asks quietly.

"I honestly don't know," James replies, his throat dry.

"Try to relax, and feel the stitching or seem on your right leg." she advises.

He follows her instructions which surprisingly eases his tension as they approach the doors dividing the male and female restrooms. A 'janitor' opens a side door just before they reach them. Miles greets the man by name, and they all enter.

"Do you trust him?" Helen continues.

"Who, Miles?" James nods toward him. "I don't remember him."

"No, I mean Pete. Why didn't he come to find you at the hospital?"

James glances back at Helen. "Pete's Mum was killed by a Horde when he was six, right in front of him. He had no other family, so I took him in. Putting him into care didn't seem right after that. He's a smart kid, did well in school, but he was drawn to the mission. I made sure he finished school and took online courses for an education, but he wanted to help. We didn't know what we were fighting at first, but with his help, we learned how to find them. As for why he didn't come

CHAPTER 15

by... well, he was following orders for once and must have gone back up the tunnel. But don't worry, he's safe."

James can't see the concern on Helen's face as they step into a large elevator. It descends for several minutes, taking them about a mile below the surface. When the doors open, they step into a bright, sterile-looking lobby with a sitting area and reception desk. The gleaming sky blue walls and clean design make it clear that this is the official entrance to the facility. A young woman in a blue suit greets them as they walk past, and several security guards in similar white attire nod in acknowledgment.

"Why does this feel like I've walked into Heaven?" James mutters.

Samantha chuckles. "Studies show sky blue relaxes people, especially government officials who've just been introduced to our existence."

The room they enter next is vastly different—more of a NASA-style control centre, with walls covered in monitors displaying news feeds and maps of various countries. Staff in military-style uniforms are stationed at computer terminals, each focused on their specific tasks. Large interactive tables display maps and videos, and the room hums with the efficiency of a well-oiled machine.

James watches as Miles speaks with several officers, signing papers and shaking hands. It takes him a moment to realize that all the staff have stopped what they're doing and are staring at him. Feeling the weight of their gazes, James follows Miles and the others out of the room and into a corridor.

"Welcome to the UK headquarters of the Council of Solomon," Miles announces with pride. "The facility has been updated since you were last here, not that you'll remember. We now have dedicated sections for communications, intelligence, medical wings, and laboratories. There's also a more advanced war room, training area, garage, and hangar, as well as the original residential and social spaces for our personnel. We've gathered technology and equipment from around the world, thanks to our ever-expanding Order and the collaboration of the greatest minds on the planet. With similar facilities worldwide, we can coordinate our mission more effectively." Miles pauses, looking back at James. "Again, not that you'll remember."

James can sense the mix of frustration and disbelief in Miles's tone. "Why do I get the feeling he either doesn't believe I've lost my memory or is angry that I can't remember any of this?" James asks Helen quietly.

"Probably both," she replies with a knowing look.

James follows closely behind Helen and nearly bumps into a man standing on the other side of the door. The man is 6'7", an Indian giant with muscles barely concealed by his casual black tracksuit. His long, wet black hair is tied back in a ponytail, and his unkempt beard suggests he's just out of the shower. Aayaan opens his mouth to greet Miles, but his expression changes when he spots Samantha. She ignores everyone and

CHAPTER 15

leaps into his arms, planting a passionate kiss on his lips.

After an awkward 30 seconds, Miles clears his throat. Samantha turns her head without pulling away from Aayaan. "Sorry, Boss, got carried away," she mumbles into Aayaan's mouth.

Blushing slightly, Aayaan gently sets her down, keeping an arm around her. He nods to Miles. "Apologies for my appearance, Miles, but I just got back. When I heard you'd arrived, I had to come. I wanted to see him."

Miles raises an eyebrow as Aayaan glances at James. Without a word, Miles walks past them and enters a nearby room.

Aayaan looks down at James, scowling slightly. He steps closer, his massive chest nearly touching James' face, and lets out a low growl. James holds his gaze, unflinching.

"Sorry, big guy, but I can't tell if I'm supposed to fight you or kiss you like she did," James says, nodding toward Samantha.

Aayaan lets out a deep, booming laugh, then effortlessly lifts James into a bear hug. James gasps. "It's been too long, my brother," Aayaan says in a deep Indian accent.

He sets James down, keeping a large hand on his shoulder. "मैंने तुम्हें याद किया मेरे भाई, old friend."

Without thinking, James bows low, then straightens up, startled by his own action. He doesn't know why he bowed or what he just said. Helen and Aayaan share a look of surprise.

"I thought you said he had no memory?" Aayaan asks Helen.

"He doesn't."

"I don't," James and Helen reply in unison.

"Come, my brother," Aayaan says, opening the massive 30 cm-thick vault-like doors. "You've been out in the cold too long, and your family awaits."

As Aayaan steps inside, James hesitates. "What did I say to him?" he asks.

"You said you missed us." Helen replies.

James takes a reluctant step forward and walks through the doors.

"Our long-lost brother has returned. James, meet the Agents of Solomon," Aayaan announces.

The room beyond is vast, with a ceiling that seems hundreds of feet high. Soft lighting mimics natural sunlight, and the walls are painted a calming sky blue. In the corner, a large willow tree grows, casting a peaceful ambiance. At the centre of the room is a large circular table, with eight people seated around it. As Aayaan's voice echoes through the room, all but one rise from their chairs and approach James.

Looking a little nervous, James steps forward. The first to greet him is Shih, a youthful-looking Chinese girl with her

CHAPTER 15

long black hair tied back in a ponytail. She wears a cashmere sweater, a knee-length skirt, long socks, and trainers. She hugs James warmly, kisses his cheek, and whispers something in Chinese. Though James doesn't understand how, he laughs at her comment.

Next is Bill, who strides over laughing, shaking James' hand and slapping his arm. He is one of the men who was with Samantha fighting Berith. Bill, no longer wearing combat clothing, is dressed like a cowboy—jeans, boots, a shirt, and a waistcoat. His belt holds two spotless LeMat revolvers. "Well damn, Jimmy, ain't you a sight for sore eyes!" he says in a thick Arizona accent.

"Thanks?" James replies, unsure.

Before Bill can continue, a voice interrupts from the side. "Let me stop you before you start another of your long, boring tales from the Old West."

The speaker is a tall, thin, pale man with slicked-back black hair and a neatly trimmed goatee. He's dressed in a black three-piece suit with a red tie, giving him the look of a modern vampire. His voice carries a Romanian accent.

"We all know about your gun slinging days, William, and frankly, we're tired of hearing about them."

"Go burn in the sun, Vlad," Bill snaps back.

In a flash, Bill draws one of his revolvers, pointing it directly at

Vlad. Simultaneously, Vlad draws two curved knives from the back of his belt. They stand, staring at each other for a tense moment, then both smile and lower their weapons. Vlad turns to James.

"You look terrible, James, more so than usual. I understand you have no memories of this," Vlad says, extending his hand. "I'm Vlad, and the cowboy is Bill."

"Vlad?" James repeats, shaking his hand.

Vlad nods. After the handshake, he pulls James into a brief hug and pats him on the back. Again, James feels a strange sense of familiarity he can't explain.

"Hello, James," Kenneth greets, standing to James' right in a perfectly tailored navy, single-breasted suit. His posture is rigid, hands clasped behind his back. Before James can respond, Kenneth is shoved aside by his identical twin, Scott, who immediately pulls James into a hug. He is the third man with Berith.

"Bro, it's about time you came back! I knew you were alive, and I kept telling them we'd find you. I just knew it!" Scott exclaims.

Despite being twins, Kenneth and Scott couldn't appear more different. Kenneth, impeccably dressed and reserved, contrasts sharply with Scott, who looks like he just rolled out of bed in his jeans, t-shirt, short-sleeved shirt, and leather sliders. Kenneth's hair is neatly styled, and he's clean-shaven, while

CHAPTER 15

Scott's shoulder-length blonde hair and scruffy beard give him a much more dishevelled appearance.

"I don't even know what to say to that," James replies, half-smiling.

"My man," Scott grins.

"Let me see him," a voice says from behind the group. It's Watanabe no Tsuna, dressed in a black suit with a crisp white shirt and black tie. He stands in front of the table, and the group parts as James nervously walks toward him. Watanabe bows low to James. He stops his bow and looks at James.

"Look at you," Watanabe says.

James stands awkwardly, unsure of what to do.

"It is good to see you, my brother. Many years have passed since we last met."

"I don't know you. I don't know any of you or any of this." James gestures to the group, then around the giant room, finally pausing at the large willow tree.

"I mean, come on. I'm in some kind of underground evil-genius lair, with a freakin' tree next to what looks like King Arthur's table. Even if I could remember, why would I want to?"

"Well we were the knights after all" Bill chimes in, pointing to the others.

"Wait, what?" James asks, exasperated.

The group laughs, guiding James to sit in one of the chairs around the massive round table. Its three-meter radius of solid marble holds more chairs than there are people in the room, but James' eyes are drawn to one across from him. The wooden chair is burned, with scorched marks stretching out onto the table in front of it. Whatever caused it was clearly violent, and James can feel the weight of its history.

The group regales James with animated stories, some spanning centuries, many involving him—though he remembers none of it. They laugh and poke fun, especially at Vlad and Bill for their recent stand-off. Despite his confusion, James can sense the familial bond among them, the warmth and connection filling the room. The only one not joining in is Helen, who remains silently distant.

"That's enough for now. You can all catch up later, and we'll explain our history in due time. For now, we have more pressing matters to attend to." Miles says, re-entering the room from a hidden door. He walks over to the table and takes a seat—his chair, notably less regal than the others.

James' gaze drifts again to the burnt chair, and suddenly, a wave of uncontrollable rage surges through him. His fists ball up, tension radiating from his entire body. Just as he feels on the verge of losing control, Helen places a hand on his, instantly easing the tension. The unexpected gesture surprises

CHAPTER 15

him, and when she doesn't pull her hand away, he turns and locks eyes with her.

They quickly realize the room has gone completely silent. Everyone, except Miles, who is busy looking over papers, is smiling at them. Scott makes a teasing kissy face at the two.

"Piss off," Helen mutters, her voice breaking the awkwardness.

Once the laughter dies down, Aayaan stands and looks at Miles. "If I may?"

Miles gives a nod of approval, and Aayaan continues. "There has been Horde activity in Pakistan, and we believe it's connected to Lilith. Several pregnant women have been abducted from their homes."

The room falls into a heavy silence.

"We've received confirmation from several sources that the Horde is about ten miles outside of Multan—possibly the Legion of the Horde called Marbas. There are no government facilities or military bases in the area, and communications from Multan have gone silent. They're clearly trying to stay hidden."

"Wasn't the Great President Marbas supposed to be hiding in Brazil?" Helen asks.

"How solid is this intel?" Bill inquires, leaning forward.

"The Middle East HQ has been investigating, but so far, only whispers. I've requested backup from Paris, but I thought you all might have better insight." Aayaan replies.

James clears his throat. "Who are Lilith and Marbas?"

Miles presses a button on his desk, and a small screen rises in front of him. Behind him, a large wall screen lights up, displaying an image of a lion with glowing red eyes next to a demonic seal with "MARBAS" inscribed on it.

"Marbas, also known as Barbas, is a Great President of the Horde. He commands thirty-six legions, though he's been steadily losing them to rival factions. Despite our efforts, we've never been able to track him down," Miles explains.

He presses another button, and the image shifts to a view of Earth, zooming out to show the moon and then zooming back in on the surface, specifically the Wargentin crater.

"Years ago, an object struck the moon. However, it didn't cause any visible damage, almost as if it had landed. NASA sent a team to investigate, but they reported it was nothing more than a meteor composed mostly of ice. Two weeks later, there was an accident at the lunar station, resulting in the deaths of three crew members. The sole survivor, Commander Sarah Lindsay, made an emergency evacuation back to Earth. A month after her return, she disappeared."

The screen displays an image of the astronaut, followed by footage of her module landing at sea.

CHAPTER 15

"After this incident, we encountered a Horde nest in Mexico. We know the Horde have experimented on humans throughout history—what people have attributed to religious sacrifices or alien abductions. But this was different. We found several young women, all in their teens, dead and strapped to beds. They appeared to have died during childbirth, but each one had severe internal burns. Their organs were completely incinerated. There were no signs of the infants."

Miles slowly rises from his seat, leaning on his cane. "We've studied the Horde hierarchy extensively, much of it documented in the Ars Goetia. They always refer to a King or Father, but there has never been any mention of a Queen or Mother."

"And the Horde that fell to Earth have never reproduced. If our theory is correct, the meteor that struck the moon wasn't just debris. It was Lilith. If they're using human women to breed, this changes everything."

James stares at the group, mouth slightly agape. "So, a meteor lands on the Moon , and now girls are turning up dead with their insides burned out. And you all think this is connected to some... mother of all monsters?"

His question lingers in the air for a moment. "Come on." James continues.

"We didn't come to this conclusion lightly," Miles replies sharply. "Some of us did not leave the Order."

"Miles, that's enough," Helen cuts in, her tone firm. "You're out of line."

"Hey, I was fine on my own. You're the one who dragged me into this circus. Just show me the door, and I will be on our way," James snaps, matching Miles' tone.

The screen suddenly changes, showing a young girl lying in a hospital bed. Her head is wrapped in bandages, and she's hooked up to machines, clearly in a coma. James stares at the image, feeling a pang of recognition.

"Susan Jones?" he asks, his voice dropping.

"Yes, James. The young girl you shot in the head," Miles responds coldly.

"We had been watching that area for weeks because we had intel there might be Horde activity. Since there was no movement and no communications, we assumed it might be where they were keeping the pregnant girls. What we didn't expect was for you to show up and blow our entire operation."

"I killed her. How is she still alive?" James asks, disbelief washing over him.

"Your interference actually worked in our favour, so credit where it's due," Miles says, a small grin creeping across his face.

"Come again?"

CHAPTER 15

"Helen was doing a routine check of the house when she saw the fight. Some might call it fate, but I think we can all agree it was just dumb luck. And for once, we got lucky. Our clean-up team found Susan under some rubble, bullet in the head and all. They got the shock of their lives when they realized she was still breathing. We have no idea what to expect, but we're monitoring her closely."

Miles pauses as a staff member quietly enters the room and whispers something into his ear. James watches as Miles' expression hardens, his gaze locking onto James with renewed intensity.

"If you'll all excuse me," Miles says to the group. "James, Helen, please join me."

They follow him down a narrow corridor and into a dark room filled with computer screens and a large observation window. On the other side of the glass, a brightly lit room reveals Pete, sitting at a table and munching on a large bag of crisps, his rucksack beside him.

Miles turns to James. "I believe this young man belongs to you," he says, his voice carrying a note of expectation.

Chapter 16

James sprints across the rooftop, dodging vents and weaving through washing lines, his eyes locked on the figure ahead. His target leaps effortlessly over an alley to the next building, and without hesitation, James follows suit. But as he lands, his ankle snaps, followed by a sharp crack in his wrist as he hits the roof hard.

"That looks very painful," a hissing voice sneers from behind him.

A clawed hand wraps around James' neck, lifting him effortlessly off the ground. The hand belongs to a middle-aged woman, her athletic frame muscular and powerful beneath her workout clothes. As her grip tightens, James struggles for air, swinging desperately at her but failing to land a single blow. She responds with a brutal punch to his face, shattering his left eye socket. Pulling him closer, she speaks.

"You're relentless, aren't you?"

Her face distorts, lips cracking as they stretch, teeth elongating into sharp points, saliva dripping down her chin. A long, warty

CHAPTER 16

tongue snakes out and licks the side of James' face as he recoils in disgust. She walks to the edge of the roof, holding him tightly, looking down at the bustling rush-hour traffic below, where street lights are just beginning to flicker on.

"Look at them down there," she whispers into his ear. "Scurrying like rats."

She dangles James over the edge.

"Tell me, rat, do you think they'll stop what they're doing to scrape you off the pavement?"

Her grip loosens, and James gasps for breath. "Kill you," he manages to croak, but her claws tighten again, cutting him off. Just then, her attention is drawn to his ankle, which begins to move and crunch as it rapidly heals. Her eyes widen in shock.

"I didn't know..."

With a powerful leap, the demon — Azazel — carries James across to the next building, crashing through a third-floor window, taking part of the wall with them. They tumble into a living room, smashing through the couch, coffee table, and TV. A young mother screams, grabbing her four-year-old son and huddling in the corner.

Azazel stands, her body shredded and embedded with shards of glass, her hair torn out in clumps. Her hunched frame surveys the room, large yellow eyes locking onto the terrified mother and son.

"You'll do," she growls.

She strides toward them, flinging the dining table aside as if it were weightless. Ripping the boy from his mother's grasp, she lifts him to her face. The mother lunges to reclaim her child, but Azazel's foot slams into her skull, crushing it instantly. The woman's body twitches before going still. Azazel turns back to the boy, her claws curling under his chin.

"Open your eyes, boy," she hisses, her foul breath hot on his face. "I want to see the light go out of them."

She raises her hand, her claws growing longer and sharper, ready to strike. But before she can, James throws himself onto her back, plunging two kitchen knives into her temple. Azazel screams, thrashing violently, tearing chunks of the walls and ceiling apart. In her rage, she rips the gas cooker from the kitchen. Blood spurts from her face as she pulls the knives free and turns on James, her shrieks echoing in the ruined room.

James pulls a pistol from his jacket, but Azazel lunges at him, stabbing her claws through his torso and sinking her teeth into his neck. He howls in pain, clawing at her, even driving his thumb into her eye socket, feeling the resistance give way as it sinks into her skull.

Suddenly, a plate smashes against the back of Azazel's head. She releases James and spins around to face the small, trembling boy, now standing defiantly amidst the dust and debris. Azazel cackles, dropping James to the floor in a bloody heap. She takes a step toward the boy, but another plate crashes into

CHAPTER 16

her face, wiping the smile from her lips.

James, leaning against a wall, spots the broken gas pipe where the cooker was ripped out, hissing dangerously. With a surge of adrenaline, he staggers to his feet, scoops up his pistol, and grabs the boy. Without hesitation, he runs past Azazel, heading for the window. Turning his back to the open air, he leaps through it, firing a series of shots into the kitchen. The last bullet causes a spark.

An explosion erupts behind them just as James and the boy crash onto the roof of a garage below, the force sending them sprawling onto a parked car. Dazed, James opens his eyes, his body already healing. The unconscious boy lies on his chest. Gently cradling the boy, James kicks open the garage door and stumbles out, looking back at the burning building. The explosion has blown off an entire wall, and flames are licking their way through the remains.

Sirens wail in the distance. James heads down a nearby alley, carrying the boy towards an unfinished building, its skeletal concrete structure standing vacant. Inside, he finds a makeshift office, lowering the boy onto the floor and using his jacket as a pillow.

James stumbles to a nearby sink, washing the blood and grime from his face, picking shards of glass from his hair. He catches a glimpse of himself in the mirror as the cuts on his face slowly close, healing as if they were never there.

A crashing sound echoes from the other room, followed by the boy's terrified screams. James bolts in, only to see the Horde standing in the centre, her body burnt and mutilated. Her skin is charred black, with only one arm left, her face ripped in half, and her jaw barely hanging on. Her clothes are nothing but scorched rags. Her laboured breathing fills the room, a rasping sound as if she's trying to speak.

The boy rushes to James, but James quickly pushes him into the bathroom, slamming the door behind him.

James turns his attention back to the struggling Horde, smiling coldly as he notices her one remaining eye widen in horror. She looks down at her feet, where her left foot is perched on a makeshift pressure plate, wires snaking from it to several barrels scattered around the room.

Calmly, James walks over to a nearby table and picks up a crude detonator. For a moment, his eyes drift to his forearms, which burn with strange, glowing tattoos—something that's happened many times before. He pushes the odd sensation aside and focuses on the Horde. She glances at his tattoos too, and for a second, James wonders if she's afraid of them. But he shoves the thought from his mind.

He glances back to the bathroom door, ensuring it's securely shut. Tightening his grip on the detonator, he looks the Horde in her mangled face.

"Any last words?" he asks.

Before she can respond, he cuts her off with a smirk.

CHAPTER 16

"Screw it."

James presses the button, and the barrels detonate, sending fire and shrapnel ripping through the room. The blast hurls the Horde into the air, engulfing her in flames. A secondary explosion rips through the ceiling, and in a matter of seconds, all five stories above collapse, crashing down on top of her. The walls, designed to withstand the force, stay intact for the most part, but the sheer weight crushes the Horde beneath the rubble.

James barely manages to escape the blast zone, turning back to see the Horde being buried alive. But as he surveys the room, he notices cracks beginning to spread across the walls. The explosions have done more damage than he anticipated.

Realizing time is running out, he kicks down the bathroom door and, without a word, grabs the terrified boy. They sprint out of the crumbling building just as it collapses entirely, burying the Horde beneath tons of rubble. As they race through a nearby alley, away from the sound of sirens closing in, James thinks he hears distant screaming from under the debris.

Finally, they reach a quiet spot, and James sets the boy down. Looking him over, he's relieved to see that apart from a few bruises, the kid seems physically unharmed.

"You're going to be okay, kid. What's your name?" James asks, catching his breath.

The boy, tears streaming down his face, looks up at James,

trembling as shock begins to set in.

"Peter," he whispers.

Chapter 17

Miles scans the report in his hand. "He got in through an emergency tunnel and hacked the security systems without us noticing, which is remarkable. We only found him wandering near the hangar by chance. For some reason, he doesn't show up on any of our cameras."

James glances through the one-way mirror at Pete, who's sitting at the table eating crisps and sipping from a can. He turns to Miles and Helen. "Has he said anything?"

"He asked to speak with you," Helen replies. "And demanded food and drink. Otherwise, he's been polite but uncooperative."

James walks out of the observation room and into the interview room. Pete, still chewing, looks up.

"Finished?" James asks.

Pete swallows and smirks. "Have you seen that futuristic-looking jet they've got in here?"

James sits down opposite Pete and takes a crisp from his packet. "What the hell are you doing here?"

"After you left the hospital, your signal started glitching. I got bored waiting and came to find out why. Glad I did."

James takes another crisp, and Pete pulls the packet back. "I gotta say, I wouldn't forget a place like this. That control room's straight out of a movie."

James leans in. "My phone was confiscated at the hospital. How did you track me?"

"They took my phone too." Pete nods at James' pocket.

James pulls out Pete's phone, sliding it across the table. Pete unlocks it, revealing a map of Glasgow with a red dot at Central Station. He presses a button, and the view shifts, showing the dot several hundred feet underground.

James looks down at his arms, his legs, then at Pete, confused. Pete smirks, nodding toward James' stomach. Instinctively, James grabs his abdomen.

"You've got to be kidding me. How?"

"Birmingham," Pete says, leaning back smugly. "After you escaped with only half your body intact and ended up five miles downriver, I figured I'd better track you. Since you wouldn't let me, I got creative. Before every mission, I make sure you eat something. The food contains a microscopic tracker. It

CHAPTER 17

lasts a few days, tops. Russian tech. I can track you anywhere on Earth, even 10 miles underground. The only thing it can't penetrate is radiation."

The door opens, and Miles enters.

"Mr. Collins, you've embarrassed several departments in this organisation, which is tasked with keeping this facility secret. We'd like to offer you full access as our guest if you can explain how you managed to get in."

Pete perks up. "As long as I don't have to wear a uniform."

"Oh, you're a long way from that," Miles chuckles.

Pete makes a snooty face to James, who shakes his head. Miles notices and clears his throat. "Come with me; I'll introduce you to the family."

Pete follows James and Helen into a large room where several agents sit around a table. As they enter, the agents stand, sensing Pete's nervousness. Helen places a reassuring hand on his shoulder.

"This is Pete," she says, calm but firm. "He's a friend of ours."

Pete looks at her, surprised.

"These are our brothers and sisters, Pete. We were together when we found the rock that made us who we are." Helen gestures to a woman. "This is Samantha. Historically, she's

Zenobia, ruler of the Palmyrene Empire in 267 AD."

Samantha steps forward. "Which means, historically, I'm a badass, and fully capable of kicking my brother's ass. Hurry up and get your memory back so you know that." She smiles warmly at Pete, easing his tension.

Helen continues. "This is Aayaan—Khalid ibn al-Walid, one of history's greatest military commanders."

Pete looks up at the towering man. "Don't let this overwhelm you, Mr. Collins. We like to show off occasionally," Aayaan says with a deep, commanding voice.

Then Bill steps forward, enthusiastically shaking Pete's hand. "William H. Bonney, but you can call me—"

Pete interrupts, wide-eyed. "Billy the Kid?"

The others chuckle as Bill clears his throat. "Just Bill. You and I are gonna be pals, I can tell."

A young Chinese woman pops a bubble of gum. "I'm Shih. Stick with me, I'll keep you straight," she says playfully.

"She's not as innocent as she looks," Helen adds with a grin. "She terrorized the China Seas in the 1800s."

Finally, a sharp voice cuts through. "Enough, child." A tall, thin man approaches, offering a bow. "Mr. Collins, I am Vlad."

CHAPTER 17

Pete leans toward Helen. "Why does he look like a vampire?"

The room bursts into laughter, except for Vlad, who sighs. "Every mortal says that."

James and Pete blurt out in unison, "You're Dracula?"

Vlad rolls his eyes. "No, I don't drink blood, and no, I don't turn into a bat."

Helen moves on, introducing a quiet man at the back. "This is Watanabe no Tsuna, the famous demon hunter from Japan."

Watanabe pulls out a chair for Pete. "Please, relax. This must be overwhelming."

As Pete sits, the others engage him in conversation. He listens to Billy's wild stories, but his attention keeps drifting to Watanabe, fascinated by his samurai past.

Suddenly, Miles re-enters, his expression serious. "I have terrible news. Patricia Gillard was murdered last night in Paris."

The room falls silent. James looks at Pete, confused, and then back at Miles. "Who is Patricia Gillard?"

Miles presses a button, displaying Patricia's image on the screen. "She wasn't an agent, but she helped us from time to time. We don't know how, but her throat was slit. There are no signs of Horde activity, but the circumstances are unusual."

James looks around, seeing the worry etched on everyone's faces. "How could this happen?" Samantha asks, her voice shaking.

Miles responds, "We don't know. This is unprecedented. Patricia showed no signs of life. I'm sorry."

The screen fades, and the room is heavy with shock. Pete, gathering his thoughts, finally speaks up. "Why can't James remember all of this?"

"Can't or won't?" Aayaan says pointedly.

James leans forward, shielding Pete from Aayaan's view. "Easy."

Helen also steps in. "James, you're safe here."

Miles, sensing the tension, speaks. "Let's try to answer that question. James, if you and Pete would follow me, we'll run some tests. The rest of you, gather information from Paris."

Miles leads James and Pete toward the medical wing, with Helen by their side. As they walk, they're met by Henri Shauss, Miles' assistant.

"It's a pleasure to meet you," Henri says in German.

"Maybe you can fill me in then," James replies dryly, also in German.

CHAPTER 17

Miles gestures for Henri to lead the way. "We'll start with some tests. Rest assured, this is one of the safest places on Earth. Pete will be well looked after too."

James glances back at Pete and Helen, offering a small, reassuring smile.

Chapter 18

Manon Bissett was not supposed to be at the Paris headquarters of the Council of Solomon today. She was called in on short notice by the French Director but doesn't know why, and at this point, it's irrelevant. The screams outside the room she's hiding in drown out the rapid beating of her heart. She struggles to slow her breathing and suspects she might have a concussion as she stares at her own vomit on the floor. She touches the back of her head and feels a lump forming. The young man in the suit who helped her into the room lies motionless, blood pooling around him.

The Director of the General Directorate for External Security (DGSE) moves to the dead man and searches his waist for a weapon. She's not surprised to find none; all weapons are checked upon arrival, and only security personnel carry them within the facility. The gunfire, which was heavy minutes ago, has stopped, and that's not a good sign as the screams continue. She also hears what sounds like screeching and laughing. A loud bang echoes nearby.

She cannot stay in this room; she needs to move. Looking around the small interview room for anything she can use as a

CHAPTER 18

weapon, she finds nothing. Holding her head again, she tries to calm herself and avoid being sick, but she fails. After a few minutes, she wipes her mouth and pinches the bridge of her nose. She moves to the door, opens it slightly, and looks up the corridor, seeing several mutilated bodies. Heads are ripped off at the neck, arms are scattered on the floor, and there is a lot of blood. Bissett ignores the carnage and spots a dead security officer several yards from her door. He is still holding a Heckler & Koch HK416 assault rifle.

Listening carefully, she doesn't hear any sounds in the corridor as all the screams come from other areas of the facility. She opens the door wider, crouches, and moves toward the officer. Trying to ignore that he's missing half his head, she unclips the rifle from the strap. She searches the officer's body for a radio when she hears a noise behind her—a low growl and the sound of bone crunching.

"Bonjour, mademoiselle. Qu'allez-vous faire maintenant?"

Chapter 19

James stands halfway down the corridor of the facility's residential section. It is intentionally decorated to resemble an upscale hotel or American apartment building, aiming to make everyone feel relaxed and comfortable. Wooden numbered doors line either side of the long corridor, and above each door handle is a fingerprint reader for individual security. James walks along the corridor and stops at door number seventeen. He doesn't know why he's here or why he has stopped at this door. The number on the door has been removed, but the outline is still visible, and a large sticker reading "ENTRY FORBIDDEN" is clearly visible.

"Why seventeen?" he mutters to himself.

He raises his hand to place his thumb on the reader but stops himself. Taking a deep breath, he closes his eyes and exhales slowly. Opening his eyes, he stares at the thumb lock for a couple of minutes. His breathing becomes heavier, and he struggles to stop himself from shaking, though he doesn't know why. He reaches out and places his thumb on the reader. A sharp beep sounds, and the light above his thumb turns red, followed by a mechanical voice.

CHAPTER 19

"Permission denied. No entry permitted. Security has been notified. Please remain where you are."

James doesn't remove his thumb.

"Damn it."

The light above his thumb turns green, and the door locks disengage.

"Voice coding and secondary thumb print recognized. Permission granted."

James instantly steps back, unsure of what to do. His hand moves from the thumb code to the handle, and he pushes the door open fully. The air inside is stale and dusty, indicating that no one has entered this room in a very long time. He steps inside.

The room looks more like the study of an obsessed historian than a place for sleeping. A single bed in the corner is more for collapsing in than for comfort. Shelves on two walls are filled with books, folders, and scraps of paper. An old, tattered wooden writing desk across from the bed has a stack of journals piled on top, with an unfinished journal open to a half-written page and a pen next to it. In one books heft is a collection of stocks and pebbles. They have all been polished and look like they have been collected from around the world. He walks to the shelf and turns a couple over with his fingers. He picks up a small reddish one and has a strange familiarity with it. He pushes the thoughts to one side. James then walks to the only wall without a bookshelf.

The wall is covered with framed photographs, capturing a lifetime. The woman who occupied this room is in almost every picture. The photos lack notes or titles, but somehow James knows when they were taken. Despite his memory being limited to 50 years, he feels a deep connection to this room and these photos.

Day 3. Helen holds their daughter in her arms, wrapped in a hooded towel and fresh from her bath. The baby is crying for milk, while Helen laughs, unable to stop. They both look beautiful to James, so he grabs the camera.

Year 6. Helen sets up a picnic with sandwiches and a freshly baked cake. James runs across the field, pretending to be chased by their daughter, who is pretending to be a monster. When she trips and falls, James lifts her and throws her into the air repeatedly. The laughter fills the air, and Helen captures the moment with her camera.

Year 11. James lands on the ground with their daughter strapped to his front, both wearing warm hats and goggles. The parachute folds onto the grass behind them. Helen runs up, kisses them both, and unclips the straps while calming the excited girl, who asks if she got pictures.

Year 13. Helen and James share a kiss by the fire at their campsite, interrupted by giggles and the sight of someone who should be sleeping, holding a camera.

CHAPTER 19

Year 21. James and Helen sit proudly among the audience. Helen has to remind James to sit down as their daughter's name is called. In a black gown, she walks to the podium to accept her qualification, giving them and a smitten Miles a tiny wave.

Year 26. James watches from the sidelines as a man behind the camera instructs a group where to stand and to be silent. Helen stands front and centre among a group of new recruits, while their daughter talks to a young man in the second row. James decides he must talk to Helen and reassess Mr. Fotheringhill's assignment to the Arctic station, making him chuckle to himself.

Year 28. Helen adjusts James' sporran, tears in her eyes, while their daughter, dressed in a beautiful white dress, laughs beside them. James thinks he should have followed through with that Arctic transfer.

Year 32. Helen and James stand at the side, watching their daughter, now front and centre, as she waits for the photographer to instruct the new recruits. They both know she can't be comfortable with the due date drawing closer.

James takes the last photo off the wall.

"I know these photos, but I have no memory of who she is, only the pain I feel..."

James slowly turns around, tears streaming down his face. He can sense Helen standing in the doorway. James stares at her, his voice trembling.

"I don't know any of this." He gestures around the room, his voice quivering with frustration. "I don't know who I am, who you are, or anyone else here."

His voice rises with anger and frustration.

"For what feels like my entire life, I have lived without understanding why I'm here or what my purpose is. I don't know why I've been hunting demons or how I've survived impossible injuries. I accepted it, but there's something more—something beyond the memory loss. Something deep inside me," he says, jabbing a finger into his chest.

"There's this great sorrow and emptiness, an unspoken pain. When I sleep, I feel like I'm falling, and a distant scream wakes me. When I'm still, my eyes fill with tears for reasons I can't understand. My body tingles with an anxiety I can't shake, and only when I'm hunting does it lessen, but it never stops. It's always there."

His legs tremble, and he collapses to the floor, his knees hitting with a crunch. Helen rushes to him, wrapping her arms around him. His cries fill the room as his body shakes uncontrollably. Helen holds him close.

"Anna Rose Fotheringill. She was only a few months old when we found her. She was the sole survivor of a battle with the Horde just outside Paris. Her parents and family were killed, and she had a head injury. We took her to the French Council

CHAPTER 19

HQ instead of a hospital to ensure she received the best care. After a few days, tests showed no lasting injuries. We tried to locate any family who could take her in, but we couldn't find anyone. We didn't hesitate. Our kind cannot have children, but it's common to take in children left behind by the Horde. We never did, thinking it would slow us down or distract us. But Anna filled an unspoken void in our lives, one we cherished with every waking moment."

Helen takes a deep breath.

"It was Astaroth."

The name hits James hard. It explains his obsession with it.

"His claws took her and our grandson's life, even before the child was born. You blamed yourself."

James stops shaking and looks Helen in the eyes.

"You blamed yourself, but it wasn't your fault, James. You wouldn't listen. You left the Order to find Astaroth, and we never heard from you until I found you in that house."

Helen relaxes her hold and gently kisses his head.

"I am sorry," he whispers.

Helen doesn't move or react to his apology.

"Your results are ready. I came to get you, but later we can talk.

I can tell you more about her."

James doesn't respond or turn around.

"I would like that."

They both stand up. James heads for the door but turns when he sees Helen still standing there.

"I didn't want..."

James takes steps to be in front of her.

"What?" James asks.

"I wasn't expecting you to be in here and didn't want to bring Anna up. Not yet."

They have moved close to each other, James takes a hold of Helen's arm and pulls her closer.

"I didn't either. Sorry if that opened old wounds."

Helen's anger flares, directed at James. She pushes him away from her.

"Old wounds?"

Her voice rises with intensity.

"Helen..."

CHAPTER 19

"You left me."

James moves forward, opening his mouth to speak.

"You left me when I needed you the most. You blamed yourself for what happened, which is fine, but did you stop to think about me?"

"I don't remember."

"Stop using that as an excuse. My daughter was murdered, and you left me without looking back or seeing how I felt. I was alone, James, completely alone."

"You had this," he says quietly.

He does not say anything further, knowing there is nothing he can say to Helen. She walks out the room. He takes one last look at the photos before following her.

The medical waiting room is painted a pale blue, furnished with a table and comfortable chairs. James, Helen, and Pete stand before it, waiting. Miles enters with the Chief Medical Officer, Dr. Sinnott, who is dressed in a white uniform, similar to the style worn by other officers in the facility. Dr. Sinnott, a very thin man with thinning hair and horn-rimmed glasses, approaches James.

"Thank you for your patience, James. We have your MRI results. Would you like to sit down?" Dr. Sinnott asks.

"If you don't mind, Doc, can we just get to it, please?" Helen says, not waiting for James. Dr. Sinnott glances at Miles, who nods in agreement.

"Very well." Dr. Sinnott walks to the large screen on the wall and taps his tablet. Several images of James' head appear on the screen, all taken from the MRI machine.

"The scans include MRI and CT scans, as well as other tests we've developed over the years. What's apparent from the initial scans is that your head is emitting very low levels of radiation, or radionuclides—three types in particular," Dr. Sinnott explains.

Pete takes a step back, giving James a worried look. Dr. Sinnott offers Pete a reassuring smile.

"Don't worry, the radiation is confined to James' skull. The radionuclides are iodine-131, cesium-134, and cesium-137, typically found in cases of nuclear power plant meltdowns. For context, anyone near the Chernobyl disaster was exposed to these substances."

"What does this mean?" James asks, looking at the others.

"Normally any radiation agents are exposed to dissipate over time. That's just the beginning of what we found." Dr. Sinnott taps his tablet, and the screen shifts to show James' skeleton, then to a faint outline of his skull and brain. A small, marble-sized object at the centre of his brain subtly glows. The three of them stare at the object in bewilderment.

CHAPTER 19

"What the hell is that!?" James eventually asks, turning to the doctor.

"To put it simply, we have no idea. It might explain your memory issues. Whatever it is, it's not being rejected or allowing your brain to heal. We're astonished you can function at all. We recommend removing it as soon as possible."

A heavy silence fills the room.

"If it's emitting low-level radiation, could it be sending or receiving any kind of signal?" Pete asks.

Dr. Sinnott glances at his tablet, then at Miles.

"I don't think you—" Dr. Sinnott begins.

"Also, if you try to remove it, is there any chance it could have a trigger device inside? Could there be a bomb or something that releases a chemical or gas?" Pete continues.

"I'm sorry, who is this?" Dr. Sinnott asks, looking at Miles.

James shifts to a defensive stance. Helen touches his arm, calming him.

"Doctor, this is Pete Collins. He's a friend and very perceptive for his age, so I suggest you address his questions. Or are you being overly defensive because you haven't considered his suggestions?" Helen says.

"Now wait just a minute." Dr. Sinnott removes his glasses, which have steamed up.

"Doctor, after conducting further tests to determine if this object is sending a signal or has the potential to explode, when can you operate?" Miles interrupts.

Dr. Sinnott takes a deep breath, mumbles to himself, and checks his tablet.

"I don't think there are any reasons to wait. We should remove it now."

At that moment, Miles' phone beeps. A worried expression crosses his face, and he exits the room without saying a word. Just as he closes the door, an emergency tone sounds through the speakers, followed by an announcement:

"This is a level two emergency. All personnel to your stations. I repeat, this is a level two emergency. All stations to their posts. This is not a drill."

Chapter 20

Miles admires the black Dassault Falcon, a triple-engine jet that has been upgraded and modified into one of the fastest and most advanced aircraft in the sky. Its stealth capabilities are enhanced by its advanced outer layer, and it boasts a hidden arsenal of weaponry. Additionally, the jet features four concealed thrusters under the fuselage, allowing for vertical flight and landing.

The Immortals, a large fleet owned by the Council of Solomon, are used worldwide by both the Order and the Council's human assault teams. Immortal 5 awaits clearance for take off. Once cleared, it will accelerate along an underground runway leading to a sloping exit at an unused area of Glasgow Airport. The Council has coordinated with Glasgow's air traffic control to ensure space for arrivals and departures.

Aayaan glances out of the cockpit's side window and gives a nod to Miles as the inner bay doors of the hangar open. The engines roar to life as Aayaan increases the throttle, taxiing the jet into position. The rear ramp slowly closes as the jet moves forward.

Miles is startled when a figure darts past him toward the jet.

James leaps for the door and clings on as the jet accelerates up the runway. He pulls himself inside just as the side cargo door closes and takes a moment to catch his breath. At the unused area of Glasgow Airport, a large patch of grass slides open, revealing a secret runway and startling a few seagulls. With a burst of speed, the jet shoots out of the opening and into the sky.

James stands, rubbing his hands, and finds himself in front of a black off-road jeep with tinted windows. The wheels are secured to the hull, and James walks past to the jet's middle section, which has been converted into a control room. The left side is equipped with chairs, computers, and communication equipment, while the right side is stocked with weaponry. Despite the lack of visible insulation on the walls, the engines are almost completely silent. Helen sits next to Shih at the communications side, focused on a monitor. Samantha, Scott, and Kenneth are also present. Helen glances over her shoulder at James before returning her attention to the screen.

"Dude, I knew you couldn't stand by and watch us have all the fun," Scott says.

Scott loads a Colt AR-15 and slings it over his shoulder. He picks up a CZ 805 Bren assault rifle and hands it to James, who smiles as he accepts it.

"Didn't hang around for brain surgery then?"

CHAPTER 20

"The alarms kind of distracted me." James replies.

"I even brought this along and customized it just the way you like it. That's if you remember how to use it," Scott teases.

James inspects the weapon, unloading and reassembling it with practised ease. Scott laughs; both he and his brother Kenneth are experts with firearms, having designed or improved many used in the civilized world. Kenneth approaches, holding out two billy clubs.

"I assume you still favour these for hand-to-hand combat?" Kenneth asks.

Kenneth hands James two black metallic sticks, each 12 inches long, with a subtle studded grip and a small indentation halfway down where the thumb would go. James swings the billy clubs skilfully and holds them in a defensive stance.

"Notice the thumb indents?" Kenneth asks.

James examines them more closely.

"Press once for one configuration and twice for another," Kenneth explains.

James presses the indent on one of the clubs once. Spikes emerge from the top, transforming it into a medieval mace. He swings the club and then presses the indent again, causing the spikes to retract. A double press on both clubs causes their tops to glow blue. James swings them again, and the hum of electricity buzzes through the air. Turning them off, James smiles appreciatively at Kenneth.

James shakes Kenneth's hand and then steps back, looking down at his attire.

"I didn't have time to change."

"We've got that covered too. Your suit is on the chair," Scott says.

James looks over and sees the black combat suit, which is tactical and combat-efficient, though it offers minimal practised since they are all immortal. The practised is only necessary to prevent injuries from stray bullets. After changing, he slides the billy clubs into the horizontal holders at the base of his back. Kenneth and Scott continue sorting weapons, while Watanabe sits quietly in a corner with his legs crossed and a sword resting over his knees. His eyes are closed as he mutters a prayer.

Helen walks over to James.

"Glad you could join us. What made you change your mind?"

"It didn't take much. Either get my brain operated on or join you guys on a mission to Paris. I left Pete with some scientists, so he's happy," James replies.

James opens his mouth to speak, but Helen cuts him off. "We can talk later. Let's focus on the mission."

CHAPTER 20

Helen places a hand on his arm, and a jolt of warmth and familiarity floods through James. He fights the urge to pull her close, his emotions clearly visible on his face as Helen withdraws her hand. Realizing his awkwardness, James tries to salvage the moment. "So, what's the mission?"

Helen brushes her hair back and turns to address the group. "Listen up."

She gets their attention and continues, "Assault Team Bravo 5 was on a mission in the Chapursan Valley, northern Pakistan. They were sent to gather intel on a previously identified Horde camp. The Council lost contact with them an hour ago. Here is their last transmission."

Helen gestures to Shih, who presses a button at the computer terminal. A recording plays:

"This is Bravo 5 Two. We have Horde contact. I repeat, we have Horde contact. They have not left this village, and they have pregnant—"

The steady voice of Bravo 5's team leader, Captain Archie McDowell, is abruptly cut off by static. Shih silences the recording and taps another button. A red-lit projection of the valley appears in the centre of the room. James steps up and, without thinking, waves his hand through the image, then catches himself and refocuses on the seriousness of the situation. The image zooms in on what appears to be an abandoned village.

"This image is live. There's nothing moving that we can see. We've also lost Bravo 5's transponder signals and their video feeds. We were lucky to get the audio. We have no additional intel on the village beyond what Bravo 5 was given. The Horde may still be here, or it could be a trap or just bad intel," Helen explains.

Aayaan's voice comes over the tannoy from the cockpit. "Get ready. We'll be in Pakistani airspace in two minutes. There's a storm approaching the target, which is both good and bad for us. Visibility will be poor, so we can't conduct re-con from above before landing, and it's going to be a bit rocky."

The jet begins to shake violently. Scott glances at James, who has moved to sit next to Samantha.

"A bit?" Scott jokes.

Samantha leans in. "I know this all feels strange to you. But you're handling it well. Once this is over, we can get that thing out of your head and be a family again."

James smiles at the woman who says she is his sister.

The Immortal 5 slows down, and four circular doors on the fuselage slide open to reveal vertical thrusters. They fire silently, and the main flight engines cut off, bringing the jet to a slow, circling flight 300 meters above the village, which contains about 15 houses. To the south is a large compound surrounded by 12-foot walls. Aayaan exits the cockpit and joins the others as Shih changes the central projection.

CHAPTER 20

"Vlad and the others have touched down in Paris," Aayaan announces.

The cabin lights go off, and a night vision green image of the village appears. Shih presses a keypad, and the image changes to show heat sources, including a few fires in houses and a truck's engine. She pauses, staring at the projection.

"No movement in the village or any heat signatures. The buildings are completely empty," Shih reports.

She adjusts the image to a deeper shade of green. "This should pick up even minor movements and show any Horde, as they won't appear in thermal. The village is completely dead."

"We should go in anyway. I want to see what's in that compound," Aayaan suggests.

Before he can continue, Kenneth interrupts. "Wait, there's movement coming from the compound. Zoom in."

Shih magnifies the projection to focus on the compound's door. Three figures move away from the door and along the village's main road. The image follows them, revealing an elderly man and two teenagers. One carries a bag, and none of them have heat signatures. They enter a building and disappear from view. Shih zooms out.

"Did you see that? They acted like they were human," Scott observes.

"This doesn't make sense. Why would three Horde walk through an empty village and pretend to be human?" Helen questions.

"I've seen this before," James says, looking at Helen.

"The house outside Glasgow— the Horde were protecting a human girl and pretending to be human. There were three Horde being unusually careful, more than ever before. I don't think it's to hide from us."

"This can't be true. Why would the Horde pretend to be human? They capture and control humans, not hide," Aayaan argues, folding his arms.

"He's right," Helen agrees. "The Horde usually hides in plain sight within high-profile settings, like governments or religious organizations, but never in a normal life. This village is isolated, and we find three pretending to be human. They know we have the technology to find them, so this isn't for our benefit. It doesn't feel right."

"The question isn't 'why are they hiding' but 'who are they hiding from?'" Kenneth suggests.

Everyone looks at Kenneth.

"What if it's Lilith? What if she's hiding from the King and his Court? Maybe there's a reason she didn't arrive on Earth with the rest of the Horde," Kenneth proposes.

CHAPTER 20

"Are you suggesting a schism? That Lilith is in hiding from the Court before even arriving here?" Scott asks.

James breaks the silence. "Wait a minute."

He steps away, raising his hands as if to halt the conversation. "Before Miles and Samantha came to my hospital room and brought me to the Council, I had a visitor. Someone who claimed his name was Valac."

The room falls silent as James continues, "He mentioned something about 'Tabula Rasa.'"

"A clean slate," Kenneth replies.

"So, what if you're all wrong? You've said the Horde wants to rule the world. The Order of Solomon has always fought to stop them, but what if Lilith doesn't want to rule? What if she wants to destroy it—wipe it clean?"

"If that were true, why create more Horde? What's the gain?" Samantha asks.

Aayaan looks up at the cabin's roof. "Did you get that, Miles?"

"That's an interesting theory. We'll look into it here. Report in when you can. I'll contact you once Team 2 reports in from Paris," Miles says through the speaker before disconnecting with a click.

"We're wasting the dark. We need to capture Lilith and then

we can ask her questions. I've been thinking about how to take the village quietly, but we don't have time or the manpower for that. I suggest we blow a hole in the front door and go in hard and fast. We can't let her escape. Agreed?"

Shih presses a button, turning off the projector and filling the cabin with red light. The others grab their weapons, and Aayaan nods to himself with pride. He loves his team. He heads to the cockpit, sits down, and turns off the autopilot. Using the throttle and elevator, he lowers the jet's altitude toward the village. Sand is blown away, and several rooftops are ripped off. One of the teenage Horde lands on the jet's nose, its skin ripped and broken. Razor-sharp talons dig into the jet to secure itself. The Horde roars at Aayaan, displaying rows of jagged fangs.

"We have company," he says into his mic casually.

A second teenage Horde slams into the nose of the jet but fails to grab on and is blown away by the sand and the jet's thrusters. A loud thump on the top of the cockpit makes Aayaan look up.

"Everyone out. Now."

Aayaan slams a button to activate the rear ramp. The five agents leap out into the wind and sand. They land hard but recover quickly and look up at the jet as it ascends and the ramp closes. With a loud boom and a wave of force, the jet propels itself forward and up into the night sky. The agents don't have time to look up any longer as shouts and roars from the compound grow louder. Weapons ready, they advance toward the compound door. Helen takes charge, moving to the front

CHAPTER 20

and using her radio to communicate over the loud winds.

"Kenneth, get high and secure the perimeter. We don't want any surprises. Shih, you go with him and try to contact Aayaan and let HQ know we've made contact. We need to ensure we still have an extraction plan. Once we're through the main doors and any resistance is neutralized, Scott, you stay in the courtyard until we can assess what's inside. They sound agitated, which might work to our advantage. Let's move."

They reach the closed double wooden door. Scott, after feeling it, gestures that it seems thick. Samantha retrieves a black breach explosive from her rucksack and hands it to Scott, who places it below the handle of the left door. Scott signals to the top and bottom of the door. Samantha rolls her eyes, pulls out two more explosives, and hands them to him. They step back, and Samantha signals for everyone to stand by.

Scott activates the remote, and the doors explode inward, taking out two Horde who were listening behind the door. The agents rush into the courtyard and, with three bursts to the head each, neutralize five Horde emerging from the main building. Samantha, Helen, and James continue forward and enter the building. Scott fires a single round from his Colt AR-15 into a Horde on the ground to his right and smiles.

"Don't move now."

The main building door is solid steel, but the Horde had left it open in their haste. The agents enter in formation but meet no resistance and hear nothing inside. The large room, the size of a hotel lobby, has only a small fire in one corner and no windows. An M2 Browning with .50 caliber rounds sits in the centre of the room, with boxes of ammunition beside it. On the wall opposite the door is an opening with carved steps leading down, lit by flickering lights.

Helen signals for the others to halt. She listens intently, then presses the earpiece mic button. "Kenneth, any movement outside?"

The reception is poor due to thick walls. "Nothing... Aayaan... Helen," he replies.

"Anyone else think this is off?" James asks.

Samantha approaches the weapon in the centre of the room, running her hand up the barrel and brushing off a layer of dirt. "This weapon hasn't been moved or fired in a long time. I agree with James, this is all wrong."

Helen moves toward the stairs and turns to the others. "If this is a trap, let's get it over with."

James walks toward her, slaps her shoulder, and heads for the first step. "And they call me impatient."

James descends the stairs with the others following. The poorly lit staircase is made entirely of stone. They travel roughly 50 yards before James stops, holding his fist up and pointing to his ear. In the distance, they faintly hear a generator and something else—babies crying. The crying is fading. Scott

CHAPTER 20

quickens his pace, with the others following closely.

They reach a landing just large enough for them. A doorway across from theirs has more steps leading down and additional lights. A generator in the corner hums, powering the area. The crying grows louder from the direction of the stairs ahead, but the number of cries is diminishing. Urgency grips the agents, but Helen leads the way, racing down the stairs without raising her weapon, bouncing off the walls as she accelerates.

Helen sees another landing approaching but doesn't stop. She jumps down the last few steps and lands in a larger room than the previous one. As she starts to stand up, she freezes in horror at the scene before her. She raises her hand behind her to signal the other agents to stop. In front of them stands a female Horde, her sand coloured robes covered in blood.

Helen struggles to process the sight of naked, bloodied bodies of white-skinned babies with their umbilical cords still attached, their heads bitten off. The Horde female grins at Helen, her mouth filled with rows of razor-sharp teeth, with flesh stuck between them. Helen scans the room for other babies but finds none. She turns her head slightly to the right, silently telling the others not to move. The Horde's long, rotting, snake-like tongue licks the face of the living baby she holds with seven taloned fingers.

The only remaining living baby, now all cried out, merely whimpers. The woman looks at the agents with glassy black eyes and laughs with a deep, guttural sound.

"Want some?" she growls, spitting blood and skin over the baby's face before biting its head off in one vicious motion. Time seems to slow for Helen as an overwhelming emotion takes over her. It takes several moments for her to realize that she has opened fire. The agents empty their magazines into the Horde female, tearing her limbs apart as she is thrown against the wall. They continue to fire, quickly changing magazines. Smoke and gunpowder fill the room, obscuring visibility.

Helen hasn't moved, still gripping her rifle's trigger until James slowly takes it from her. She jumps at his touch, looking down at her empty, bright red hand, veins bulging from the pressure.

James places Helen's rifle over his shoulder and guides her to the steps they came from. He motions for her to sit down and takes out a bottle of water and a rag. After wetting the rag, he dabs Helen's face, cooling her down. He doesn't say anything, knowing he wouldn't have the right words but understanding exactly what she is reliving.

Samantha approaches the pile of mush that was once the Horde and looks at the bodies of the babies, breaking the silence. "I don't understand this. What are we missing?"

James looks at Samantha and notices something above her head. "Look."

James points to a small, dirty speaker bolted to the wall.

"Welcome and thank you for coming."

CHAPTER 20

The voice crackles and distorts, but James and Helen instantly recognize it as Astaroth's Russian accent. The voice jolts Helen out of her shock and makes her stand up.

"I'm sure you have many questions, but save your breath since this has no microphone. I'm guessing you're all here, except for Kenneth, Scott, and Shih, who are still on the surface. The others must be in Paris, which will be fun for them. To make things fair, I'll give you 60 seconds. The countdown has started, so I'd start running if I were you."

A click comes from the speaker, followed by a countdown tone. The agents don't waste time questioning each other and race up the stairs, clearing them two or three at a time. They know they need answers but can't afford to be buried under tons of sand. They sprint past the .50-caliber machine gun and burst out the doors.

"I repeat, this is Samantha. We need an immediate extraction at the compound."

The agents run out of the compound to find Scott waiting outside. They stop several yards past the door, bending over to catch their breath.

"What the hell is going on?" Scott asks.

Kenneth and Shih join them, both puzzled. James takes a drink from his bottle before handing it to Samantha.

"It was worse than we thought," James says, glancing at Helen, who still looks pained. The distortion of speakers around them makes the agents form a back-to-back circle, weapons ready. Helen, now focused, hears Astaroth's voice again, this time with an English accent.

"I wish I had cameras to see you all. Missed a trick there," Astaroth says.

The agents stand ready, scanning for any sign of the jet. Samantha looks to the sky but sees nothing.

"Now that you've had a nice run and are clear of that horrible compound, we can get started."

A loud boom erupts from the compound as it explodes, and the agents watch as it disappears into the sand. The ground shakes with the explosion.

"MOVE!" James shouts.

The ground starts to swell, growing and consuming the village. The agents turn and sprint in the opposite direction. Samantha hears crackling in her ear and pushes her earpiece in further.

"Stand...i...5....conds..."

She would recognize that voice, no matter how distorted it is. Suddenly, the Immortal 5 appears overhead and lands in front of them, crushing several huts under its wings. The agents run for the rear bay, which was open before the jet's wheels hit the ground. Scott, the last agent aboard, shouts into his ear

CHAPTER 20

that they are in. His eyes widen as the ground collapses toward them. He grabs onto a handle as the Immortal 5 lifts off the ground but stops a foot above it.

"Left wing!" Aayaan shouts through the speakers.

Scott stands at the end of the ramp and looks over, seeing that the wing is caught under a water tank next to one of the collapsed huts. He lifts his foot to swing around and climb onto the wing when a hand grabs him. He turns and sees Samantha, who motions for him to move. She raises an M203 grenade launcher with a modified grip for single use and aims it at the wing.

"As soon as you feel the shake, punch it," she says.

Scott shouts into her ear, grabbing onto her flak jacket. Samantha squeezes the trigger. The 40mm explosive round launches into the water tank, destroying it. The jet bursts into the air with a shudder. Losing her grip, Samantha begins to fall toward the expanding hole, while Scott tightens his hold. They both watch as the grenade launcher falls and disappears into the dark cloud of sand. The jet lifts off and rockets into the night sky.

Chapter 21

"We are approaching Paris. Any contact from HQ, Helen?" Aayaan shouts through the cockpit door.

Helen looks at Shih, who shakes her head while listening through her headphones.

"Nothing. I can't even tell if our signal is being received. It's like we're sending it into space," Helen replies.

She turns to the others, who are still dusting off sand and drinking water.

"Miles reported losing contact with Team 2, and HQ received Paris's automated emergency signal. They're not getting any response, so we can only assume the worst," Helen says.

"Does anyone else sense a pattern here?" Scott asks.

"I agree. We should head to Glasgow immediately," Kenneth suggests.

"No, Miles has been explicit about heading to Paris. If this is a

CHAPTER 21

pattern, it started there," Samantha explains.

"I agree. Aayaan, Kenneth, Scott, Shih, and I will take the jet into the hangar. James and I will HALO onto Gare Du Nord. It's getting dark, so we should be covered for our landing," Helen instructs.

As Helen gives the instructions, the jet begins to tilt to gain altitude. HALO, or High-Altitude Low Opening, was developed in the 1940s and 1950s to deliver personnel and supplies into combat zones from high altitudes, opening chutes as low as 3,000 feet. Despite the height reaching up to 45,000 feet, special breathing equipment is usually worn, but this isn't an issue for the Agents.

"Are you sure that's wise? Wouldn't it be safer for one of us to go with you? No offence, James," Kenneth asks.

Before James can respond, Helen answers, "They might not know that James has returned to the Order. It could be useful."

Aayaan's voice comes through the speakers. "Approaching drop target in 60 seconds. Get ready."

Helen checks her equipment, including her earpiece, and picks up a helmet. She helps James into his gear, then walks to the rear of the jet, passing the secured jeep. James follows as the bay door opens. Wind rushes into the compartment, causing them to hold on tight. The jet, still gaining altitude, moves farther from the land below as the city lights shrink.

"Just remember what I told you and follow my lead. Get ready," Helen shouts into her mic.

A red light above their heads turns green, and without delay, Helen and James jump. They tuck their arms to their sides and dive rapidly. The wind roars around them as the ground and the roof of the train station come into view. Timing the jump perfectly is crucial to stay invisible to anyone below and avoid crashing through the roof.

Without the standard HALO equipment, they rely on a small device in their flak jackets that sends a small electric charge to signal when to deploy their chutes. Helen opens her chute milliseconds before James, and their descent slows rapidly. At just under 3,000 feet, they hit the roof with a thud and a snap as the wind pulls their chutes in a new direction. They slap the central button on their chests to rip the chutes, which quickly flap down. The time from chute opening to ripping is brief. Helen and James scan their landing zone, ensuring it's secure. Weapons raised, they remove their helmets.

"Team B secure," Helen says into the mic attached to her hidden earpiece.

"Roger, Team B. Radio silence from here on out," Shih replies.

Helen lifts her Heckler & Koch G36 rifle and looks at James. "Ready?"

"You lead, I follow. Before we go in, though, I need to say something about what happened in the compound. I know

CHAPTER 21

how hard that—" He places a hand on her arm.

Helen looks at him, her face softening. "Damn you, James."

She leans over and kisses him softly on the lips. He kisses her back. When she pulls away, she smiles and then playfully punches him where she kissed. It's not hard enough to knock him off his feet, but it does whip his head back. Rubbing his chin, he smiles at her.

"Seems fair. Let's go."

They move in a nearly instinctive formation toward an air vent. Helen bends down, removes a panel to reveal a metal handle with a combination dial underneath. She enters a six-digit code, pulls the handle out a centimetre, and turns it 180 degrees clockwise. The sound of a bolt unlocking echoes as the entire air vent pops up slightly. Helen pushes it open on its hinge, revealing a ladder leading down a dark shaft.

"A light should have come on, even if the power is out," Helen says.

"That's not suspicious at all. I know I have no memory of this, but does all of this seem a bit off to you?" Samantha asks.

Helen glances at James. "It's what Astaroth said outside the compound that I can't shake. Why is he back? He's never been this significant to the Horde. You spent all that time searching for him with no luck, and now we can't get away from him."

The two Agents enter the shaft.

The Immortal 5 lands vertically and taxis into the old, unused hangar at the far end of Charles de Gaulle Airport's terminal building. The jet stops, and the hangar doors close automatically. As the engines shut down, the rear ramp opens, and the Agents disembark. This is not how the Order of Solomon's aircraft would typically enter a headquarters, but with the main hangar's power down, there's no other option. The ground next to the hangar drops to expose a runway leading under the airport and to the facility beneath Gare du Nord train station.

In the rusted metal hangar's corner is a shed. To most, the old wooden shed with a rusty, unlocked padlock would seem ordinary, and that's the point. The wooden outer layer conceals a twelve-inch titanium core with stairs leading down. The lock has a combination dial like the one on the roof. The structure is designed to withstand most assaults, but with no power, things look grim.

Samantha turns the combination lock several times until a click signals the door's release. She opens the door, revealing a dark staircase.

"No lights. This isn't looking good," she says.

Aayaan walks past Samantha, inspects the dark doorway, then turns to Shih. "Head to the main power generator and find out why there's no power. Call in when you get there. The rest of us will head through the hangar and sweep the main complex. We should meet with Helen and James coming from the other

CHAPTER 21

side. Call out any targets and, until we know for sure, assume everyone is hostile. Lethal force is a priority."

Shih exits the hangar without a word. The main generator is located within the airport grounds, away from the train station, but at this time of night, there should be few workers to notice them. The access door is at runway One.

Aayaan, Samantha, Kenneth, and Scott enter the shed and descend the stairs. The torches on their rifles cast only limited light ahead, and the only sound is their footsteps. The stairwell is maintained every two months, so encountering anyone is unlikely, especially with no power. After several flights, they reach the bottom and open the secured door, leading to a dark section halfway along the runway. The main runway lights activate only when a jet is taking off or landing, but secondary lights for visibility are usually on. Tonight, the runway is completely dark.

"Sam, take point. I'll cover the rear," Aayaan orders.

Each Agent trains their rifles ahead, using the light to guide their way. They push on, aware that whatever awaits them in the main facility isn't good news. They move toward the hangar, where they spot the Immortal 5 at the edge of their torchlight. The jet is parked and dormant, which is unusual. In emergencies, Immortals are put on standby power for a quick lift-off, but there's no power, not even in the cabin lights.

Samantha sweeps her torch across the ground at the main doorway leading to a corridor. She then checks above her for any signs of trip lasers or explosives but finds none.

"Anyone else's Spidey sense tingling?" Scott asks.

"It's a little too quiet," Samantha agrees.

"Trap?" James asks.

"If it is, they're really bad at hiding it," Samantha replies.

Samantha turns around and sees Aayaan slowly approaching the jet.

"Aayaan, what is it?" she asks.

The others turn toward him.

"I heard something," he answers.

He slowly stalks to the front of The Immortal, keeping his BCM RECCE-14 MCMR Carbine aimed at the nose. He feels the unsettling sensation of being watched but can't pinpoint the source. It has been a long time since he's felt this way. The muscles on his face twitch, but he stops himself from smiling. The thought almost makes him laugh. A sudden movement on the right wing snaps him out of his thoughts, and he aims his weapon. Three shots ring out, and a body falls at his feet. It's a child. High-pitched laughter echoes from different directions in front of them.

"Orphans. A King is here!" Aayaan shouts to the others.

CHAPTER 21

He trusts his team to watch his back as he approaches the body and shines a light on it. A ten-year-old girl lies motionless. He uses his foot to flip her over. The face isn't that of a girl but a cracked, twisted visage with an unnervingly large, shark-like smile that remains even in death. There are three perfect bullet holes in her temple.

A Horde King can create what the Order calls orphans—children infected by a King's blood to become drones. Taking down an orphan is challenging, even for seasoned Agents. The laughter is the child's soul screaming from within. Killing Horde is one thing, but killing children is something else entirely.

Samantha, Kenneth, and Scott keep watch as Aayaan examines the orphan's body. He crouches down and notices something with a blinking light in the child's hand.

He manages a single word. "RUN."

The orphan explodes in a ball of fire, sending flames and debris towards The Immortal, engulfing Aayaan in a blaze of fire and metal. The Agents at the entrance are thrown off their feet, crashing through the doors and slamming into the corridor walls. The impact breaks bones, and the hangar's double doors slam shut.

Scott stands up, his vision blurred from hitting the wall and blood in his eyes. He holds his rifle with his only working hand, using the torch to reveal silhouettes of small children rushing toward him, accompanied by high-pitched laughter.

Leaning against the wall to support himself as his left ankle heals, he fires his weapon, hitting several targets before they reach him and his wounded team. Samantha, still on the ground, joins Scott in firing and slowly gets to her feet. Her left shoulder hangs at an odd angle, and she slams it against the wall to relocate it into the socket. She pulls a large piece of the Immortal from her thigh and drives it into the temple of an orphan who has broken through the gunfire. She bends down to check Kenneth, seeing his head is badly injured.

"We can't stay here. Push forward to find an open door, and I'll bring Kenneth," she shouts to Scott.

Scott puts some weight on his healing ankle and limps up the corridor, finding an unlocked door. He pushes it open, comes back, nods, and stands guard as Samantha pulls Kenneth in. Scott follows and secures the door, locking it in place.

"How is he?" Scott asks.

Samantha unclips a torch from her belt and shines it on Kenneth's face and head. His skull is already mending, and the bleeding has slowed. The door shakes from the banging outside.

"I will be...fine," Kenneth slurs.

"My man," Scott whispers.

"Check your weapons. We can't be boxed in here," Samantha says.

CHAPTER 21

"You ready?" Scott asks.

"The explosion from the Immortal sealed the hangar doors shut, so we can't go back that way. When we leave this room, we need to go left," Samantha explains.

"Did you see Aayaan before we got thrown out?" Scott asks.

"No," Samantha answers quietly.

"So, I take it our element of surprise is gone?" Kenneth asks, slowly standing.

"I don't think we ever had one. They knew we were coming," Samantha says.

The banging stops, and Scott puts his ear to the door. "That's our cue. Let's go."

Kenneth is a bit unsteady on his feet. He aims his Saiga 12 shotgun at the door and shines its torch on Scott, who holds up three fingers. Scott counts down and pulls the door open. Samantha leads, training her MPX Pistol Caliber Carbine into the corridor and illuminating it slightly with her torch. The hall is empty, and she waits for Scott and Kenneth to exit the room.

"That isn't worrying at all," Scott comments about the empty corridor.

"On me. Eyes up," Samantha commands.

The three Agents move slowly down the corridor, which is splattered with blood on the walls and floor. There is no sound now, no more laughter from the orphans. They know they're being watched and that an attack is imminent, but they cannot stop. They must push on. Kenneth tries to contact Helen and James, but the explosion seems to have damaged their earpieces. They reach a T-junction and point their lights in both directions as well as behind them.

"Left leads to the training and residential units. Communications and the War Room are to the right, but first, there are the panic pods. We check them first," Samantha advises.

Each main section of the Council Facilities contains three Panic Pods—secure rooms designed for use during an attack. Each pod is stocked with enough food and water to last three months, can sleep 20 people, and includes a small armoury and communications system. They also have their own independent power supply. There has been no signal or messages from them, not even the standard automated distress beacon.

Without a word, the Agents head towards the first pod before reaching Communications. The door is open, and the room is completely destroyed. Every bed is torn apart, and the weapons and computer equipment are wrecked. Blood drips from the ceiling, runs down the walls, and pools on the floor. Whatever did this lost its temper. Scott points his light to the floor and sees spent shells scattered about. Whoever died here put up a fight.

They leave the doorway and move towards a large hole in the

CHAPTER 21

wall where the doors to the communications centre used to be. Someone has fired an explosive round from inside the room. They enter and scan the room, surveying smashed computer terminals, overturned chairs, and cracked or shattered monitors. The Agents move silently, scanning behind every obstacle in their path.

Laughter comes from behind them at the door, and they pivot, lighting up the entrance. Standing in the doorway is an orphan—a child, about seven years old, with slumped shoulders and long, dirty blonde hair covering its face. It sways back and forth almost trance-like. The laughter stops. Slowly, it lifts its head, revealing a large, cracked smile through its hair, and lets out a long, low chuckle.

"What's the plan here, Samantha?" Scott asks quietly.

"We need to push on. No sudden movements," Samantha replies.

The lights from their weapons stay focused on the doorway, but their senses cover the whole room. The chuckling multiplies as more orphans emerge from behind the first one. They don't cross into the room but fill the corridor, creating a mob. Kenneth's light stays on the door while Scott and Samantha scan the rest of the large room.

"What do we call a group of orphans again?" Scott asks, not bothering to keep his voice low.

"Was it a mob?" Samantha replies.

"I believe we agreed on a swarm of orphans. They act like locusts, but we chose not to name them after any animal. James coined the term 'orphan' in the early 1500s, give or take," Kenneth explains.

Like the UK facility, this room spans four floors with views of each level. Every floor has windows looking into the communications room. More orphans cram into each room, pressing against the glass and causing it to crack.

"That glass isn't going to hold them," Kenneth says.

"Fuck this," Scott exclaims.

"Yep," Samantha agrees.

Scott fires at the windows above them, followed by three shots into ten orphans, then changes his magazine and puts down another ten in seconds. Samantha draws her second MPX Pistol Caliber Carbine from behind her waist and fires 60 rounds at the doorway, taking down more orphans while Scott reloads. A large pile of bodies builds up at the doorway, but more orphans continue to push through. Kenneth aims his Saiga 12 and fires 30 rounds into the offices, shattering glass and causing orphans to fall like rain.

"We can't stay here!" Kenneth shouts, not in panic but to be heard over the noise.

Samantha changes her magazine and, before firing another round, shines her torch around the room. All she sees are

CHAPTER 21

orphans, closing in from all sides.

"Last mag!" Kenneth shouts.

The lights on their weapons reveal orphans surrounding them. They are being overrun and don't have enough ammunition to keep the swarm back, let alone fight their way out. Things are about to get messy and cramped. Samantha unclips her rifle, letting it fall to the floor, and draws her sidearms, emptying them into the nearest orphans. Before she can reload, a small, overweight thirteen-year-old male orphan crashes into her, knocking her to the ground. As it laughs in her face and claws at her, Samantha grabs it by the hair, yanks a clump out, and uses her other hand to push its grinning face away. Kenneth kicks the orphan aside and moves to hand-to-hand combat after finishing his last round. Samantha gets up and kicks away an approaching orphan. The three Agents stand back-to-back, facing and fighting off the surrounding group. Every blow drains their energy as they struggle to see a way out amid the sound of laughter.

Suddenly, the orphans stop advancing. Those close to the Agents are knocked down, but when they notice the others have stopped, they cease their attacks.

"What the hell?" Samantha says out loud.

The unbroken lights turn on, causing the Agents to slam their eyes shut and face the floor. The orphans remain motionless, heads slightly raised and eyes rolled back. As the Agents adjust to the sudden brightness, they see the carnage in front of them—bodies of orphans covering the floor and workstations.

"I hope my children haven't been too overwhelming," a deep, low, raspy voice booms from every direction.

"They do get very excited."

Chapter 22

The Agents tense, raising their weapons as they scan the room, trying to locate the source of the voice. Suddenly, they spot Echo, her body hanging over the window ledge, covered by a large, clawed blue hand. The massive, naked figure holding her nearly fills the window, making Echo appear like a doll. The beast has bluish-grey, smooth skin rippling with muscles and veins. Its pointy ears and strikingly attractive face are framed by long black hair tied in a ponytail. James can't shake the image of a genie who has spent years in the gym and taken steroids like candy.

"I believe this meat sack belongs to you," the blue creature says.

Echo is dropped onto a pile of orphans, unmoving. Scott moves towards her, keeping his weapon trained on the creature. The Agents open fire as the massive figure jumps from the ledge and lands heavily in front of them, shaking the floor. Bullets tear into the creature's torso and face, but it remains unfazed. It raises its hands and shakes its head, signalling them to stop firing. They comply but keep their weapons ready. They have never encountered a Horde like this before.

"Paimon," Kenneth says.

The Agents exchange quick glances before focusing back on the creature. Paimon takes a short bow, extending his muscular arms and spreading his claw-like fingers. He grins, revealing sharp, pointy teeth. The name has been known for centuries, often considered a myth.

"Your reputation certainly precedes you, Agents," Paimon says, his yellow, lizard-like eyes gleaming with hunger. "I have watched your Order for a long time—Order of Solomon, or is it the Council of Solomon? I get a bit confused. Have you read Solomon's Ars Goetia? It's very dull with no plot twists, though I do like the bit where it makes me a King of Hell. Has it been your idea or his to make us Demons of Hell?"

Paimon laughs, his voice filling the room as he circles the Agents, like a predator stalking its prey. The Agents track his every movement, ready to act.

"I'm sure you have many questions and an urge to attack, but I must ask you to hold both. I want to savour this moment a bit longer. The destruction of your secret, or should I say the Council's secret bases, has been planned for quite some time. It needs to be appreciated."

He pauses, waiting for the realization to sink in.

"Bases?" Samantha asks, breaking the silence.

"Don't get too caught up on that, though I have another

CHAPTER 22

surprise for you. You'll also want to know about the delightful Shih. She was very quick on her feet and almost made me drop to a knee. Alas, she will never be the same again," Paimon says with a smile.

The Agents look down at Shih, her head crushed beyond recognition. Scott supports her neck, his expression lost as she fails to heal. Her face and head are covered in dark grey dust, like soot. The Agents turn their fury back to Paimon.

Paimon grins. "Come on!" he taunts.

Fuelled by rage, Scott leaps at Paimon but is swatted away like a fly by the creature's left hand. He crashes to the ground, hard. Kenneth goes high while Samantha moves low, striking Paimon simultaneously. Kenneth's sweeping kick to the back of Paimon's leg forces him to one knee, while Samantha's roundhouse kick connects with his jaw. They roll away, creating distance to regroup. Paimon, not phased, spits dark red, oily blood on the ground.

"My turn, meat," Paimon growls.

Despite his size, he moves with surprising speed, lunging at Kenneth and slashing his chest with claws. He lifts Kenneth off the ground and uses him to strike Samantha, who tries to help. Paimon slams Kenneth to the floor and kicks him across the room. Stunned, Scott hurls a piece of wall and a computer screen at Paimon, but it's not enough. Paimon lunges through the debris, grabbing Scott by the throat. His massive fist rains down blows on Scott's face, turning it black and blue with blood.

Samantha jumps onto Paimon's back, digging her fingers into his eyes. Paimon roars in pain, dropping Scott and reaching back to pull Samantha over his head. He grips her by the waist and pulls her face close to his. Samantha punches and claws at his hands, trying to loosen his grip. Despite the blood streaming from his eyes, Paimon grins.

"That wasn't very clever, was it, meat?" he taunts.

Suddenly, the ceiling in the corner of the room explodes, causing a large section to crash down and crush dozens of orphans. Dust fills the room as Paimon throws Samantha aside like a rag doll. She lands heavily on her back, the impact knocking the wind out of her. James falls through the hole, landing on the ground with blue, electric light flashing around him. Nearby orphans come out of their trance and turn toward the light, almost mesmerized. They laugh excitedly and slowly move toward the light, which begins to swing and smash into them. Another dark shadow drops to the ground and starts firing rounds into the orphans.

"Catch!" Helen shouts.

Helen throws a large holdall to Samantha, who is struggling to her feet. Samantha places the heavy bag on the ground and opens it to reveal three Heckler & Koch HK416 assault rifles. She slides one to Scott, who can only see through one eye, and then to Kenneth, who is waiting. Samantha readies her weapon, observing the blue electric light smashing the orphans' faces

CHAPTER 22

with intense force and speed. James finishes off the last orphan with his billy clubs, and they regroup.

"Friend of yours?" James asks.

"Well, well, well, the wanderer returns. The second part of our grand plan" Paimon's deep, booming voice fills the room, surprising James and Helen.

"I think he's talking to you, man," Scott says.

"Is that who I think it is?" Helen asks.

Paimon paces side to side, his large teeth gleaming.

"You played your part well lost one, i must thank you." Paimon muses.

The others are startled by this and turn to James. It is Helen who speaks first.

"I was suppose to find you. The house, Smith, even the Mimics. We have been manipulated from the start."

"Wait, that can't be true. I have no memory of any of you before now, how is that possible unless. The Horde have been feeding Pete intel on where to go, where to strike." James says.

"Lillith!" Helen shouts at Paimon.

The others are still trying to catch up. Paimon helps them

along.

"We had to change our ways. We have been on the defensive for so long, hiding in the shadows but have never beaten you. We needed your Order focused, and distracted." Paimon explains.

He lets out a laugh.

"A "mother of Demons" He mocks.

"How very original of us, even the pregnant meat was perfect. Our Father has beaten you and your kind will finally die."

Before James can speak, Paimon cuts him off.

"Enough talk. Tear them apart." Paimon orders.

The orphans surge toward the Agents. James uses his billy clubs to fend them off while Kenneth helps with hand-to-hand combat to conserve ammunition. Helen, Samantha, and Scott fire their weapons, holding the orphans at bay. Paimon watches with interest.

"What does the rest of the place look like?" Samantha asks.

"No sign of anyone, not even a limb. The whole place has been ransacked," Helen answers.

"There weren't any of these kid things anywhere else. Looks like they were all drawn here," James shouts.

CHAPTER 22

An orphan leaps into the air and grabs James by the shoulders. Before it can bite him, its head jerks backward and explodes.

"Focus!" Helen yells, pointing her weapon at him.

"I couldn't agree more," Paimon shouts into the crowd. He charges forward, throwing orphans aside, their laughter turning to screams. He grabs James by the jacket and lifts him off the ground.

"How's the head?" Paimon asks.

Without answering, James flips his billy club around and stabs it into Paimon's mouth, letting it go. An electric surge fills Paimon's mouth, the pain causing his eyes to widen painfully. James uses his feet to push against Paimon's chest, kicking off and flipping through the air. He springs back at Paimon, who is staggering in pain, and swings the other billy club with electric force into the side of Paimon's head.

Paimon staggers, half his head burned and caved in. James swings again but is too late. Paimon, now fully focused, punches James square in the face, sending him flying back into the others.

Paimon pulls the billy club from his mouth, careful not to touch the still-charged end. He drops it and relocates his jaw, wincing from the burn.

"I am impressed. You nearly had me there," Paimon says.

Helen helps James to his feet. The Agents prepare for the next attack.

"We need to get out of here." James shouts.

"I am going to strip the flesh from your bones, over and over again," Paimon threatens.

Suddenly, the side of Paimon's face explodes, causing him to stumble and roar in pain. The Agents spin around to see Aayaan, severely injured and burnt, standing at the door to the Communications room. His clothes have melted to his skin, exposing muscle and bone. He holds a Russian RG-6 Grenade Launcher in his only fully formed hand; his right arm is a smouldering stump just past the shoulder. Aayaan fires three more rounds at Paimon, slamming him into the wall and creating a dent. The Agents rush to the door toward Aayaan, with Echo over Scott's shoulder.

"Down the corridor. Do not stop," Aayaan strains through a burnt throat.

Samantha stops in front of Aayaan, takes the grenade launcher from his hand, and touches his face with a comforting smile.

"You need a shower," Samantha says, wrinkling her nose as she sniffs around Aayaan.

James helps Aayaan by taking his arm, supporting his weight, and guiding him out of the room with the others.

CHAPTER 22

"Come on, toastie. You two can catch up later. You can't talk right now anyway with your larynx messed up. Which, frankly, we'll all enjoy," Samantha adds, causing Aayaan to cough, which James interprets as a laugh.

The group moves slowly down a corridor away from the room that nearly became their tomb, passing doorways and pools of blood. With the lights now on, they see the full extent of the attack, though there are still no bodies. The laughter from the Communications room fades as they distance themselves. The Agents check every corner and opening but find no more hostile.

"Run, Agents, go home. While it's still there," Paimon's distant voice booms.

They finally reach the hangar, using a hole in the door caused by Aayaan's grenade launcher. They climb the stairs they used to enter the base and exit into the old hangar. Exhausted, injured, and confused, they load Aayaan into the Immortal Five and strap him and Shih into fold-down medical pods. Samantha sits by Aayaan's side, watching as robotic arms inject pain medication. Scott works on a computer connected to Shih's pod, scanning her head. The scan reveals extensive damage caused by Paimon. An alarm goes off in Shih's pod, drawing Samantha's attention. A clear cover envelops the pod.

"What is it?" Samantha asks.

Scott examines the screen, which is flashing warnings. The radiation symbol appears, followed by the results.

"It's detecting radioactive material on her head—the dust, to be precise," Scott reads.

In the cockpit, James climbs into the pilot seat while Helen takes the co-pilot seat. They ready the jet and taxi it out of the hangar as the doors automatically open. As the Immortal prepares for vertical flight, a large explosion erupts at Gare du Nord airport, filling the sky with bright light. The ground begins to rumble as James and Helen work to get the Immortal into the air. Just as the jet lifts off, flames engulf the hangar.

"Hold on!" James strains.

He pulls the controls to one side, causing the jet to bank left away from the hangar as flames consume it. Another explosion erupts at the entrance to the airport's hidden runway. James struggles to control the Immortal as the shockwave from the hangar hits them. Helen adjusts the controls, pushing more power into the thrusters.

"Go. NOW!" Helen shouts.

James thrusts forward, and the Immortal rockets into the sky. He pulls back on the controls, lifting the jet into lower orbit. The Immortal speeds across the sky Northwest toward Scotland.

"We have stealth, but it won't matter. Anyone with eyes will see us shooting away from the airport. They blew up the facility," Helen says.

CHAPTER 22

"What now?" James asks.

Kenneth enters the cockpit and gazes out at the stars.

"I've been trying on all frequencies, but there's no reply from Glasgow. Aayaan is being patched up, but he has a lot of internal damage, so that's taking priority."

"How is Shih?" Helen asks.

Kenneth looks at Helen, his eyes focused.

"I suggest you come back and see," he replies.

Helen stands, placing a hand on James's shoulder and giving it a reassuring squeeze before leaving the cockpit with Kenneth.

"No, I don't have a clue how I know how to fly either," James mutters to himself.

Helen approaches Shih's pod.

"She isn't responding, and her pulse is very weak, almost non-existent. Her skull is crushed, causing massive damage to her brain. I've reattached her eye and her jaw is broken in several places. She isn't healing at all. The sensors picked up traces of radiation around her head, from the dust," Scott reports.

"Wait, did you say radiation?" Helen asks.

"Yes, very low levels, but the pod activated its safety protocol,"

Scott confirms.

"Can you identify the type of radiation and the readings?" Helen continues.

"Not from here, but I've sent the results to Glasgow."

"Have we had any contact yet?" Helen asks Kenneth.

Kenneth, engrossed in the radio station, doesn't hear the question. Scott shakes his head to respond for his brother. Helen moves to a station and presses a button.

"James, we need to get back as fast as you can. Do what you can," Helen insists.

"Should he even be flying with his lack of memory?" Scott asks.

Helen doesn't answer. She walks back to Shih's pod and glances at Aayaan, who is now talking to Samantha, who is wearing a headset to hear him. Helen looks down at Shih and knows that healing from such severe injuries will take time, but there should be some improvement. She can't shake the feeling that this is connected to James in some way.

"Two minutes!" James's voice crackles over the tannoy. Helen glances at the speaker and stands up, walking over to Kenneth. She lifts the left side of his earphones.

"Get ready. We're approaching the airport and coming in fast,"

CHAPTER 22

she says.

Helen heads into the cockpit and her eyes widen in shock. Instead of seeing an aerial view of Glasgow Airport, she sees an almost face-on view of Glasgow city centre—coming at them very quickly. She hears herself shout James's name, but he doesn't respond.

The Immortal Five plummets towards the city, getting dangerously close to Central Station. The roar of the thrusters struggling to slow the jet echoes through the cockpit. The stealth capabilities of the jet are pointless as people on the streets below look up and see the futuristic aircraft hurtling towards them. People heading home from work, shopping, or dining run in all directions, panic-stricken. The Immortal suddenly pulls its nose up, and the tail jet thrusts at full power, causing people below to cover their ears against the deafening noise. Glass windows in nearby buildings shake and nearly crack, while some cars collide as drivers try to avoid pedestrians.

Hovering over Gordon Street, at the main entrance to the station, the engines adjust for the close proximity of the surrounding buildings but manage not to strain too much. The jet's braking thrusters set a new record for efficiency, which, if anyone had noticed, would surely be noted in training manuals.

"What the hell was that?" Helen gasps between deep breaths, picking herself up from the floor. James avoids her gaze as shouting from the others comes from the cabin.

"You do understand the meaning of 'stealth jet,' right?" Helen demands.

"We don't have time for this tiptoeing around after—"

BOOM!

Chapter 23

Glasgow Central train station explodes beneath them with such force that the shock wave slams into both sides and the belly of the Immortal, cutting off its engines and hurling the jet into the Grosvenor Building across from the station's main entrance. The impact takes out the top three floors of the building. The jet lands belly up on the crushed structure, while one of its wings breaks off and lands a block away.

The station and the entire block it occupied—filled with businesses and retail shops—are swallowed by the ground. Cars, taxis, and buses are flung into nearby buildings, some soaring tens of feet into the air. People who aren't caught in the initial blasts are thrown and shattered by the explosion's force.

For a few minutes, the air is filled with the blare of alarms and the wail of car horns as dust clouds the city. Fires break out in shops and car engines. Cries for help and screams emerge from people trapped in cars, buildings, and under rubble. Emergency sirens approach in the distance.

In the Grosvenor Building, the Immortal lies like the carcass of a massive beast—broken and battered. Helen, thrown into the cabin, opens her eyes. Amid the blinking red emergency lights, she sees Shih's pod above her. It's still strapped in but powerless, with its glass shattered. Helen is on the ceiling of the jet. Samantha helps a bruised Aayaan, who has been thrown from his pod, to his feet.

"Report," Aayaan's voice cracks with his newly healed larynx.

"We need to get out of here. Now," Helen says, searching for an exit.

Kenneth climbs over broken equipment that has fallen onto the ceiling from the rear of the jet. "Bay doors are jammed shut. No exit there."

Scott stands up from behind debris, blood streaming from a laceration on his left temple, his left cheek and eye beginning to bruise. Kenneth looks at his brother with concern.

"I'm okay, just a little spacey. Can we get out through the cockpit?" Scott asks.

"I don't know. I got thrown into here," Helen replies.

Helen makes her way to the cockpit and returns quickly. "We can get out that way. James must be checking if the path is clear. Let's go."

On a side street near Central Station, a boarded-up café that has looked derelict for over ten years stands. It has never opened, and rumours suggest that after a family purchased it, a divorce

CHAPTER 23

led to a prolonged legal battle, leaving it locked. In truth, the café's sign and metal panels are a façade. Inside, what looks like an empty café with dust-covered furniture hides a steel door at the back—known to the British Order of Solomon as Emergency Door Five, one of many exits from the facility.

Central Station lies several feet below ground. Emergency services are working to rescue those trapped. Scott and Kenneth follow Helen through an alley behind the building where the Immortal crashed, carrying Shih on a stretcher. Samantha and Aayaan take up the rear. They have two handguns and a rifle between them. The Immortal Five's armoury is severely damaged, and the fate of the aircraft can wait. They reach the café, blending into the chaos around them. Using a hidden lock disguised as a defibrillator, they open the door and slip inside. The empty room, about five meters square, has low lighting and appears undamaged by the explosion. Kenneth and Scott gently set Shih down.

"Should we go find James?" Scott asks.

"No, we won't be able to in all this," Helen responds.

"Even just one of us?" Scott persists.

"Once we secure Shih, we can go back out. We need to check for survivors below," Helen answers.

"But he doesn't know where he's going."

"Dammit, Scott, don't you think I know that?" Helen snaps,

losing her temper. Silence fills the room.

"One thing at a time," Helen eventually says.

Helen turns the circular mechanism of the vault door, and Samantha helps her pull the thick metal door open. Inside, Samantha flips an old switch, powering up the corridor. Signs of structural damage are evident, with light fittings on the floor and cracks in the walls, but the corridor appears clear. The facility is circular, with corridors radiating from a central area. Though the main facility is quite a distance below, the access ahead should lead them there. At a junction, they choose to go left, preferring not to split the group. They cautiously advance toward the facility's centre but are met with a collapsed ceiling.

"We should have gone right."

Scott hears himself and raises his hands to apologize, which is accepted. They double back and continue forward, following the lights down a corridor with more structural damage and some water leaking from the walls. The place is eerily silent, and James is noticeably absent. The Agents are accustomed to James not being in their lives but always expected his return. They never anticipated he would come back in such a condition or that everything would go wrong so quickly. Despite their experience with global chaos, this situation feels different.

No one feels James' absence more acutely than Helen, but she buries her emotions and focuses on their immediate situation.

Panic rooms, or "Mines," are situated within every section

CHAPTER 23

of the facility. Each Mine can hold twenty-five people and includes catering facilities for three months, communications, an armoury, a library, and exercise equipment. They were designed with the hope they would never be used, and until now, they haven't been.

"Mines Five and Six are the closest. We stick together and stay in sight of each other—no wandering off. That means you, Ja..." Helen catches herself before she finishes the name.

"I'll take point," Samantha offers, helping Helen move past the awkward moment. The Agents continue along the corridors, carefully turning at each junction. They turn another corner and see a yellow flashing light further down the corridor. Samantha signals for them to stop and moves forward alone. She peers around the corner, rifle ready, and advances quietly. The door to Mine Six is open, with the emergency light flashing. Inside, she sees the upper torso of a woman lying at the door, the light illuminating the blood with each flash. Samantha scans the room with her rifle, turning on her torch for better visibility. She signals the others, who then enter the Mine.

After a few minutes, Samantha and Helen exit Mine Six, breathing heavily. Helen wipes her forehead, smearing blood from her hand.

"They didn't get a chance to close the doors. We counted thirteen bodies, but there may have been more. Arms, legs— everything has been torn apart. Whatever did this acted with rage and ferocity," Samantha reports.

"This is the same as Paris," Helen responds.

The others exit the Mine.

"How did they know to get to the Mine, or even into the facility in the first place?" Aayaan asks.

"That's not the first answer we need," Kenneth replies.

Aayaan looks at Kenneth in surprise.

"We need to find any survivors," Kenneth continues.

"Let's push to the next Mine. Five is nearby," Helen says, cutting off further discussion.

The Agents find Mine Five secured and breathe a small sigh of relief. Aayaan approaches the palm print security console at the large door and presses his hand against it. The computer lights up, and lines of text scroll across the screen. The screen prompts for a passcode, which Aayaan enters. He waits as another passcode, entered by the Mine's occupants, authorizes his. The sound of large pins sliding out of the lock is heard, and the door slowly swings open. Light from the Mine pours into the corridor, causing the Agents to shield their eyes momentarily. They see an elderly man with a cane emerging, his expensive suit ripped and covered in blood. Miles' face is bloodied, staining the bandage on his head. Seven other people follow him out, each with their own injuries.

"Good evening, my Agents," Miles greets.

CHAPTER 23

Helen moves to him and takes his arm, noting the cuts on his hands and examining his head.

"I'll be fine. Report," Miles says.

"He's not fine and needs to sit down before he collapses," a French voice interjects. A round-faced, red-cheeked man in blue shirt and trousers, clearly stressed by his large frame, exits the Mine. Dr. Lawrence Jean walks over to Miles with a red medical bag, wiping sweat from his forehead.

"He has a cut on his forehead and a mild concussion, but the stubborn man won't sit down. You won't be reporting anything to him until I confirm he doesn't have a concussion," Dr. Jean continues. He then sees Kenneth and Scott gently setting down the stretcher and approaches Shih to examine her. An eighth and final survivor exits the Mine, coughing and cradling his right arm in a sling, covered in dust and bruises.

"Where is he? This is by far the worst day I've had since meeting that prick," Pete says, looking past the other Agents.

"Miles, what happened?" Aayaan asks, ignoring Pete.

A young female technician re-enters the Mine, sets up a chair beside Miles, and helps him sit down slowly and painfully. He smiles at her with a resigned expression and takes a deep breath, patting her hand.

"You heard me say no reports, right?" Dr. Jean complains.

Miles ignores him.

"It happened just after you left for Paris, which I assume didn't go well judging by Aayaan and Shih," Miles begins. "Anyway, I went back to my office to change clothes, but before I could get my jacket off, I heard screaming, followed by a familiar screech. Gunfire soon followed. Vlad joined me right away and led me towards Mine One. We didn't make it—Vlad was attacked by five Horde in Order guard uniforms. They weren't new; I even wrote a recommendation letter for one of their children to go to university in America last month."

Miles pauses.

"I headed straight for the War Room. Someone needed to get word out about what was happening. When I reached the War Room, I saw—" He trails off.

"Miles?" Samantha prompts.

Miles lowers his head, breathing heavily. Just as Dr. Jean stands to attend to him, Miles holds up a hand to stop him.

"I'm fine, Lawrence," he says, taking a breath and continuing.

"When I reached the War Room door, I saw Billy in the centre. He had three Horde with him, and my guess is he was purging all three when it happened. One of them must have been booby-trapped with a bomb. When Billy started, it went off. He was containing the blast inside his energy bubble, but it wasn't enough. The wind was strong within the room, and electricity

CHAPTER 23

was shooting off in all directions. Billy was shouting at me, but I couldn't hear him. I think he was telling me to get out, but I just couldn't hear him. Pete pulled me from the door, and along with the people you see here, we somehow made it to this Mine. The Mine shook for a full minute before we lost main power. Backup power kicked in, and a few hours later, you arrived."

"Have you had any contact with Vlad and Billy?" Aayaan asks.

"As I said, the last time I saw Vlad was outside Mine One. As for Billy, I'm afraid he's still in the War Room," Miles replies.

"From what we saw above, he's buried under tons of rubble. Central Station is gone—along with the whole block. I'm surprised this area has survived," Aayaan says.

"Your turn," Miles prompts.

Aayaan glances at Dr. Jean, who just shrugs.

"We were in the Immortal above Gordon Street when the explosion occurred. It threw us into the building opposite, and that's where we lost James," Helen explains.

"What do you mean, 'lost James'?" Pete asks.

Helen approaches Pete, gives him a reassuring hug on the shoulder, which he accepts, and explains, "He was piloting the Immortal at the time. We haven't seen him since."

"Could he still be in the plane?" Pete asks.

"I was in the cockpit with him but got knocked into the cabin when we crashed," Helen says.

"We checked, Pete. We came straight here through Emergency Door Five," Scott adds, turning to Miles.

Helen's body goes rigid as if jolted by a surge of electricity.

"What about your tracker, Pete?" Helen asks.

Pete nervously pulls out his phone, which is cracked and damaged.

"OK, we can't stay here. We need to update the Order. We'll set up a temporary base of operations in the Café and take it from there. Scott, Kenneth, I need you to check the other Mines for survivors. Helen, Samantha, check what's still operational in the facility for transport and weaponry. We've been attacked, and I don't think the Horde will let up. The rest of you take Shih and get back to the secondary site. Be careful."

Miles smiles at Aayaan, relieved that he has taken charge. Despite his attempts to appear in control, it's clear he isn't in a state to lead.

Two hours later, the "Café" near the wreckage of the train station is bustling with activity. What was once an empty space is now a hub of operations, with workstations, laboratories, seating areas, first aid stations, and a storeroom full of sup-

CHAPTER 23

plies. The temporary facility is fully operational, and its staff is hard at work.

An hour after arriving, Kenneth and Scott return with three IT technicians, a nurse, and a chef, all from Mine Three. Others were either destroyed by the Horde or crushed in the explosion. The technicians are working to contact other Order facilities, investigate the attack, assist the injured, and plan their next move. Miles sits on a chair—though he would prefer a bed, he lost that argument—and watches his team work. Aayaan approaches him.

"You're doing well at staying where you are and not getting involved," Aayaan says.

Lost in his thoughts, Miles takes a moment to acknowledge Aayaan's presence.

"Excuse me?" Miles says.

Aayaan smiles.

"Dr. Jean isn't happy you're not lying down and keeps reminding me that, when it comes to medical protocol, he outranks you," Aayaan says with a grin.

"Well, as I've repeatedly told the good doctor, I don't care," Miles replies.

"You've always been stubborn. From the age of seven, people called it headstrong, but I know better. It's stubborn," Aayaan says.

"I prefer headstrong. Now, help me up. I've been sitting here too long and have seized up," Miles laughs.

Aayaan extends his arm, which Miles takes. The large, muscular Indian man knows not to pull Miles up but rather support him carefully. He hides his concern for his old friend, who looks not only tired but also much older than he did just days before. They walk to the refreshments area, and Aayaan glances at Shih, who remains unconscious on a bed while Scott sits beside her.

"There must be a pattern to all this. First Patricia, now Shih," Miles muses.

"We need to find it, or this won't end well," Aayaan replies.

"Have you heard from Samantha?" Miles asks.

"Nothing yet," Aayaan answers.

They approach a computer station where a technician is focused on Pete's mobile phone, now connected to the terminal with wires. The technician doesn't notice them at first. When she finally sees Miles and Aayaan, her loud scream draws everyone's attention in the Café. She jumps, almost falling off her stool, but Aayaan catches her just inches from the ground. She looks into his big, brown eyes, amazed, as he lifts her back onto her seat.

CHAPTER 23

"I—your—wow, I'm sorry, muscles, oh my god," she stutters.

"Are you okay?" Aayaan asks.

"Yes, sir," she manages, still mesmerized by him and holding his hand. Realizing this, she lets go, blushing.

"Please, just call me Aayaan," he says.

"Right, yes, Sir Aayaan. I mean, Aayaan sir. Aayaan, just Aayaan," she stammers, wishing she could disappear.

"Mind if I interpret?" Miles asks.

The technician turns and sees Miles for the first time, standing.

"Sir, my apologies," she says, standing up.

"Relax, please. How are you getting on with Pete's tracker?" Miles asks.

"It's annoyingly banged up, but we think we've got it," she replies.

Pete approaches, holding two cups of coffee and chewing a biscuit. He hands one cup to the technician and offers her a chocolate biscuit with a small, smitten smile.

"Ann and I managed to repair the phone as best we could. We were just about to turn it on to see if the tracker is still active," Pete says.

"Then please, don't let us hold you back," Miles says.

Pete and Ann exchange nervous smiles. Ann taps on her keyboard, presses the final keys, and holds her breath. The phone turns on, and the screen displays its contents. Ann moves her chair aside, and Pete takes her place, entering commands as if he were using the phone. A map appears on the phone, showing Central Station.

"That's the last place I checked for James. It might take a moment to ping from the cell towers," Pete says nervously.

The map zooms out to show all of Glasgow, then moves slightly south to East Kilbride, then to Carluke, and finally Edinburgh. Pete frantically taps keys, his nerves showing. Ann leans over and places her hand on his shoulder, causing him to lose focus briefly. The screen goes blank. He clears his throat.

"Sorry, give me a sec," he says.

The map reappears and continues moving south, slowly crossing the border. It zooms in past Carluke again and moves through Covington. Pete turns to Miles, puzzled.

"He's on a train," Miles says.

Pete stands up, looking at Aayaan, who remains a silent, statuesque figure behind them.

"Ann, could you confirm all the stations this line stops at and where it terminates, please?" Aayaan asks, his tone less

CHAPTER 23

friendly.

Ann nods, no longer blushing, and pushes past Pete to her computer.

"There are no trains scheduled for that line at this time. However, freights travel up and down this line to a supply station ten miles south of London, which then connects to a line to France," Ann informs them.

Miles walks away from Ann and Pete, and Aayaan follows.

"What's wrong, Miles?" Aayaan asks.

"This doesn't feel right. Why a train?" Miles replies.

Aayaan ponders for a moment. "We can ask those questions when we get there."

Helen and Samantha enter the facility, covered in dust and grime.

"We can't reach Vlad or Billy without machinery. The hangar has been destroyed," Helen says.

"We might have transport. The prototype NLJ-010420 is in the support hangar on the south side of the airport. It was moved from the facility hangar last week for further tests," Miles explains.

"We move out in ten," Helen orders, not waiting for Aayaan's response.

Chapter 24

The four-carriage train slowly travels through the small countryside station without stopping, its horn sounding. Passengers on the platform barely notice it. From the outside, it looks like a standard freight train with typical markings and serial numbers, blending in with other trains running up and down the country.

This "Hidden Freight" is used by several organized crime gangs in the UK and even Europe to transport all sorts of cargo. It is never stopped, boarded, or searched by authorities. Each carriage can be modified to specific needs, and they don't have to match. With internal and external cameras, the Hidden Freight operates without a driver or support staff, always controlled off-site. Only those hiring it have access, and every corner of the train is covered by cameras.

A guard in carriage four removes his hand from his ear and places it on the ladder leading to the roof hatch just as the entire carriage explodes, tearing it from the tracks. An alarm blares throughout the Hidden Freight.

A guard in carriage three looks at the gap where the gangway to carriage four used to be and sees only tracks. He turns to the guard behind him as two large spears burst through the roof, one skewering his colleague, the other narrowly missing him. Cables attached to each spear extend from large holes in the roof. The guard ignores the chaos and presses his earpiece.

"They're here," he shouts over the noise before being pulled off his feet and hurled into the night.

The NLJ-010420 matches the speed of the Hidden Freight, hovering twenty feet above carriage three and tethered by cables. Samantha swings into the doorway from the roof, followed by Helen. Both Agents wear the same torn combat gear from their last mission, unable to salvage anything else after the crash and destruction at the facility. They each carry a Heckler & Koch HK416 but no side arms.

"Two guards down," Samantha reports into her ear.

"Acknowledged. You have less than ten minutes before we pass another station," Aayaan responds from the NLJ.

Helen removes the sidearm from the skewered guard and hands it to Samantha, who checks it and places it in her holster. Helen moves to the doorway leading to carriage two.

"Did you hear that guy shout into his radio?" Samantha asks.

Helen turns, tilting her head. "Why aren't we being rushed by more guards?" Samantha continues.

CHAPTER 24

"Something isn't right. This carriage has two guards and nothing else—just their chairs. I'd bet the next one is the same," Helen says.

"I'll go one further and say there are no other guards. It's almost as if they knew we'd take out the end carriage," Samantha responds.

"I have no patience for this," Helen mutters to herself before turning to the door again.

Samantha and Helen go through the door and cross the gangway into carriage two. They move through the empty compartment, tense and frustrated by the growing strangeness of the situation. They reach the door to carriage one. Helen pauses, takes a deep breath, then opens it and trains her weapon forward.

Carriage one is unlike carriages two and three. Although they can't be sure, carriage one seems to be empty as well. The compartment is in complete darkness except for a beam of white light illuminating a table with a large red button in the centre.

On the button is the word "PRESS."

Helen tries to see into the darkness but can only make out something large at the end. She walks over and inspects the button.

"Ready?" she says over her shoulder.

Without waiting for a response, she presses the button. The entire compartment floods with light, forcing them both to shield their eyes and stumble back slightly. After a few moments, as their vision adjusts, what they see shocks and confuses them.

A large cylinder, roughly five feet by three feet, sits on the floor. The cylinder is filled with a red liquid. Floating almost weightlessly in the middle of the container is a left arm, from shoulder to hand. Helen instantly recognizes it as James' arm. The liquid is blood, and there must be about ten units of it.

Helen raises her weapon and fires a burst into the cylinder, shattering the glass. Blood pours onto the floor, along with the arm. She picks it up and looks at Samantha.

A beeping sound starts from the walls, resembling a countdown. They move quickly through the carriages, not looking back.

"Aay, get ready to detach the cables!" Samantha shouts into her earpiece.

In the jet above them, Aayaan hears the urgency in her voice and places his hand on the cable release button.

They reach carriage three and swing onto the roof one after another. Just as they reach the cables, carriage one explodes in a blinding white light. The cables detach as the jet pulls up and away from the blast. The NLJ-010420 speeds up, loops back around towards the Hidden Freight, and fires two air-to-

CHAPTER 24

ground Brimstone missiles at the remaining carriages, sending them off the tracks and into the surrounding fields before they reach any civilization.

Aayaan points the NLJ towards home and sets it to autopilot. He sends an encrypted message to emergency services about the explosion, warning them of hazardous materials. He then leaves the cockpit and makes his way to the rear of the jet. Being a prototype, the jet has minimal standard equipment in its main compartment. Several seats and a central unit, meant for a digital display but covered with a tarpaulin sheet, serve as a table.

Aayaan joins Scott and Kenneth, who are staring at the arm now on the table. He then looks over at Samantha, who sits with her head in her hands. Helen returns from the back with two bottles of water and hands one to Samantha.

Aayaan examines the arm more closely, lifting it up and turning it over. His eyes widen when he sees writing carved into the inside of the forearm. He runs his fingers over the words in disbelief. The alarm from the cockpit interrupts him, and he gently places the arm down, as if it might shatter, before heading back to the cockpit.

After several minutes, he returns.

"They're all gone," Aayaan says.

Samantha looks up, her face filled with concern. "What is?"

"Every Council facility around the world has been destroyed. All at the same time. Every. Single. One."

Silence fills the room as the gravity of the situation sinks in.

"Casualties are unknown currently. Arrangements are being made for any active teams we can reach to conduct reconnaissance, but that will take time. We've been severely crippled. We need to take a moment and plan our next steps."

Helen stands up and glares at Aayaan with intense determination.

"It's simple. We kill every one of them."

She covers James' arm but glances again at the words carved into it.

"SO MUCH FOR IMMORTALITY."

Chapter 25

The Clavicula Salomonis, loosely translated as "The Key of Solomon," is a book compiled from various manuscripts. Through various sources, it is said to have the power to summon and capture demons as slaves. However, this is not entirely accurate. There have been several versions of this book, or Grimoires, and the original texts were derived from notes created by King Solomon during his reign in Israel.

Solomon originally created these pages to help him understand what he referred to as "Monsters from the Sky," whom he named Demons or the Horde. He used the manuscript to devise a strategy to combat them, akin to planning an invasion of a country.

Solomon did not come up with this plan on his own. It began after a night of great rain and the birth of his second child. While waiting in his chambers, Solomon was attacked by a servant who killed fifteen of his men before badly wounding him. During the attack, Solomon realized that this servant was not a man but a demon in human guise. The attack was stopped by two warriors who entered the palace. Solomon witnessed the warriors defeat the demon and, in a flash of lightning and thunder, make it vanish. The warriors also healed with astonishing speed.

Grateful for their help and the celebration of his child's birth, Solomon convinced the warriors to stay. They grew to respect him and eventually revealed the truth about their immortality and the Horde. Over time, more warriors came to Israel and explained the threat the Horde posed to the world, insisting that it would not stop until it was destroyed. The Horde disregarded borders and rulers, necessitating the gathering of all nations to confront them.

King Solomon established The Order and dispatched his warriors to warn other rulers around the world about the Horde. For centuries, The Order, now known as The Order of Solomon, kept the Horde at bay, concealed in the shadows. Although the Horde would occasionally infiltrate civilizations or governments to sow chaos, they were always subdued by The Order.

That was before.

Chapter 26

James feels the drugs coursing through his body. His head is heavy and floppy, and he has been grinding his teeth. He tastes blood in his mouth. He cannot feel below his neck but senses he is vertical. The room is pitch dark.

He is also naked and cold.

"I see you're awake."

The unfamiliar voice sends a chill through his body.

"You've been out for some time and will take a while to recover. It's been a long time, and I believe you go by James these days."

James tries to speak but slurs out an incoherent sentence. His lips are numb, and he struggles to swallow saliva.

"That was just awful to listen to. Best leave the talking to me and just listen."

The voice is closer, coming from behind him.

"I like the new name, by the way. It suits you. We have much to catch up on, but I'll skip that and tell you what you've missed since you were picked up. The last thing you'll remember, of course, is the crash of your fancy jet. Well, your base of operations has been destroyed, as have all the Order's facilities worldwide. The Order is no more."

Feeling returns, moving down his body.

"The Horde set a trap that you and your friends walked into, and you were the key to all of that. This setback has pushed the Order back by centuries. Anyone in positions of power who had knowledge has been wiped out, and I don't think you'll find another Solomon anytime soon."

He can feel the breath on his left cheek. Whoever this is, they are very close. A long taloned finger runs down James' face.

"Just as I foresaw. It is time for my children to rise."

After a long silence, James realizes that whoever it was is now gone. He regains feeling in his limbs. They are bound, and he feels intense pain in his left arm from shoulder to hand. He can also sense the skin growing over muscle. His entire arm has regrown, indicating he has been unconscious for at least a week.

"Mind your eyes, James," a different, deeper voice booms. This voice is familiar. Paimon.

James squeezes his eyes closed just as the light flicks on. He

CHAPTER 26

slowly opens his eyes and focuses. He is in a room so white it's almost disorienting, making it hard to discern where the floor meets the walls and ceiling. He looks down and confirms he is naked.

Heavy breathing behind him sounds almost like a gorilla.

"How do you feel?" the voice asks, with an almost growling undertone.

He tries to turn his head, but it is bound to the table. Paimon sniggers and walks around James.

Towering over him, Paimon's chest is puffed out, and his arms hang like tree trunks. He is wearing a black suit with a white shirt and black tie. His skin still blue. James fills his mouth with saliva, feeling how dry his tongue and throat are. He badly needs a drink.

"Nice suit," James croaks.

Paimon smiles and looks down at his attire.

"Do you like it?"

Paimon turns, showing off his look.

"I'm applying to be a member of the Order of Solomon. You are in dire need of new recruits after all." he laughs.

James' eyes focus more, and he sees that the suit is not clean or new. It is torn in places and covered in blood. The suit doesn't fit Paimon; it's too small for his large frame. He has taken it from someone.

"The former owner didn't need it any more, so I carefully removed it. I think I look pretty good. The hole in the back is a bit breezy, but that's what happens when you remove a man's spine."

Paimon turns, revealing the ripped hole in the back of his suit. He laughs, then tears the suit from his body, shredding it to pieces. Rolling his shoulders back, he takes a deep breath, causing his body to grow. Claws burst from his fingers, and his new height and build almost fill the room. His shark-like grin spreads across his face.

"Much better," he growls.

James feels his strength returning and his senses sharpening, but he knows that even if he were not tied to the table and at full health, this hulking figure would still overpower him.

"Why do I have to be naked?"

Paimon ignores the question and paces in front of him, hands clasped behind his back. James tries to maintain eye contact.

"You and your kind have been hunting us for a long time. We've always hidden in the shadows, afraid of being caught, always on the run from you. Your powers and annoying ability to heal from anything have always given you the upper hand. We've

CHAPTER 26

never had a way to stop you."

Paimon stops and turns to him.

"That all changed with our incredible discovery."

"You do know you have said all this already, and it was boring the first time.

Paimon moves closer to James and leans in, inspecting his right forearm. The tattoo that winds around it begins to glow. His left arm glows slightly, still healing. James sees this but there is no pain in his head like before. The longer Paimon stares at it, the brighter it becomes. His face strains, and his body tenses until he pulls away and stumbles backward. The glow fades, but James feels the power he has drawn from Paimon has bolstered his strength. Paimon bends over, spits on the ground, and laughs.

"I didn't think that would happen in your condition. Still got a fight in you. It's a shame that memory has quite come back, you might know what all this means. I see you are no longer having headaches."

This jolts James. Paimon knows about the headaches. He knows that whatever power the others make knocks him out. Paimon puts his hand in front Of James. He is holding a grey marble and it is making James feel slightly light headed.

"We removed this from you whilst you were unconscious. It has done it's job nicely, leading us straight to their home. A very clever thing it is but you do not need it now."

He takes it away, taking away the sick feeling. Paimon throws it away like it is nothing and smiles at James.

"So weak."

Paimon turns his back to James.

"Untie these straps, and I'll show you how weak I am" James replies, trying to sound defiant.

With great speed, Paimon moves to James and grabs him by the neck, lifting him and tearing the bonds from the table. He squeezes James' throat, causing his eyes to widen.

"Do not tempt me, meat. If you were of no further use to us, I'd tear you apart."

Paimon throws James across the room. He crashes into the wall and lands on his front. Pain shoots through his body, sapping the strength he had just regained. The restraints have come loose, but the weight of the table pins him to the floor. He hears a door open and Paimon's footsteps retreating.

"Get him into a chair and bring him out. His audience wishes to see their contender."

James is lifted into the air by two Horde members he hadn't seen enter the room. They drag him through the door and drop him into a wheelchair. A large shutter opens, flooding

CHAPTER 26

the room with light. The deafening applause hits him as he focuses on the scene before him. The room is filled with a massive crowd surrounding what looks like a colossal Mixed Martial Arts cage, five times the size of a standard octagon, resembling the ancient Roman Colosseum. The crowd's cheers are not for him but for the spectacle. Thousands of levels rise to a stone ceiling. The air is thick and toxic, making James cough.

His wheelchair is pushed down a long ramp and into the centre of the octagon. The two men tip him out of the chair and onto the ground before exiting, leaving the cage open. James struggles to his hands and knees, catching his breath. Out of the corner of his eye, he sees someone walking into the cage. The figure in a bright pink suit bends next to him.

"Catch your breath, James. You're going to need your strength," says a voice like nails on a chalkboard. It's Astaroth.

Astaroth stands and walks away, addressing the crowd.

"Ladies and gentlemen, WELCOME TO FIGHT NIIIIIIIIIGGGG GGGHHHHTTT!" he shouts into a microphone.

The crowd erupts into a frenzy.

"We have been hunted and forced into hiding for too long, but tonight, you will all witness the new dawn of the Horde."

More applause follows.

"We will take our fight from the shadows. We will bring our fight to their door. They have been crippled beyond repair. We have struck at their heart and soul."

James listens to Astaroth but remains focused on finding a way out. He needs to understand what has happened since he was taken and how long he has been held.

"For centuries, we have hidden within kingdoms and governments, bending them to our will but always remaining behind the curtain, out of sight from their saviours. Their protectors."

Boo.

"Their Council."

Boo.

"Their Agents."

Boo.

"Their Order of Solomon!"

The crowd shrieks and roars. Astaroth knows how to stir the crowd and where his speech is headed. He turns to James.

"Agents like this one," Astaroth says, stretching out his arms dramatically.

Finally, James nearly says to himself.

CHAPTER 26

"All of you will recognize this Agent. Most of you have seen him in action. We took his memories, but not his thirst for revenge. Give it up for our first-ever contender, the enemy of us all, the worst father in history. The one. The only. The man now known as JAMES!" He draws out the name.

James stands on shaky legs and glares at Astaroth, who basks in the crowd's adulation, arms outstretched and head held high. The crowd, entirely Horde, is not hiding in human form. Their hunger to tear him apart is palpable. Escaping won't be easy.

As Astaroth enjoys the applause, James channels all his strength into a sudden attack. He grabs Astaroth's jacket, lifts him over his shoulder, and slams him against the cage. Astaroth quickly jumps up, holding his hand out in front of him.

"Don't be too premature, James."

James tenses, ready for an attack that never comes. Astaroth glances behind James, who tilts his head. Just as he suspects a trick, he hears footsteps approaching. James turns as a slim, gangling Horde runs into the cage. James drops to his back, using the momentum to kick the Horde over his head. The Horde nearly collides with Astaroth, who leaps out of the way and exits the cage, slamming the door behind him. He doesn't stop as he runs up the ramp and disappears.

Before the Horde can fully recover, James leaps and strikes it in the face with a knee, shattering its nose. He follows up with three more knees and a kick to the side of the head. Dragging the Horde to the centre of the cage, he straddles its chest and pounds its face with punches. He feels bones crunch under his fists.

Still leaning over it, James concentrates, trying to recall Helen's actions and feeling a burning in his arms. Almost instinctively, he stands, stretching out his arms. His tattooed forearms blaze with bright light. Wind swirls around him, forming a ball of electricity mixed with white flames. The gravity within the cage seems to pull toward the ball as James gathers energy, bending and crossing his arms into his chest.

BANG

He collapses to the ground, feeling the energy coursing through him. The bullet hitting his shoulder and interrupting the process. He looks up at the crowd, breathing heavily. The overwhelming presence of the Horde almost overwhelms him.

The room falls silent before erupting into roars and cheers. The crowd is thrilled by the spectacle. Music blares from speakers, and lights flicker on.

"My Horde, look at that! What a start! Let's get the next fight underway," Astaroth's voice booms through the speakers.

James watches the ramp as lights from the ceiling illuminate two large Horde emerging. The bullet in his shoulder dropping to the ground as his shoulder heals. Faster than ever before. Was the marble slowing his healing process, is this what it feels

CHAPTER 26

like to be whole?

The Horde walk closer. One has massive claws and a mouth full of teeth. The other is solid muscle, with hands the size of James' torso, and appears to be made of stone. The crowd cheers for their warriors.

A section of the floor beside James opens, revealing a table. Ignoring the posturing of the two "gladiators" outside the cage, James walks over to the table. It holds a Buck 119 Special hunting knife and a standard black katana. He inspects the knife, ensuring it is sharp and balanced, before tossing it to the corner of the cage, where it sticks into the floor. He picks up the katana, examining it closely. Despite its simplicity, it seems in good condition. Underneath the katana, James spots something he hadn't noticed before: an M67 frag grenade.

He almost laughs, placing the katana back on the table. He picks up the grenade, pulls out the pin, and holds onto the clip, facing the cage door.

The Horde stands at the door, growling at James. They want in and could force their way, but they are bound by the rules. The cage door opens automatically, and James lets go of the grenade clip. The Horde with claws rushes in on all fours, charging at James. As it nears, James jumps aside and throws the grenade into the Horde's mouth. The creature skids to a halt, turning to face James. James rolls away, realizing he's moved further from the table and the katana. The other Horde struggles to enter the cage due to its size.

James glances at the floor, then at the Horde, and smiles. The Horde notices the grenade pin and clip on the floor and its eyes widen.

It lunges at James, claws extended, but before it can reach him, a loud boom erupts. Its head and upper torso explode, scattering debris around the cage. James brushes teeth and skin from his hair and face as he stands up.

Amid the crowd's shouts and roars, a deep laughter resonates near him. He turns and sees the second Horde, which has entered the arena. It laughs at James, shaking its head as if James has made a grave mistake. This massive creature, slow but powerful, points at the katana and throws it at James' feet, nodding its head eagerly.

James' shoulders slump, and he curses under his breath. He despises being toyed with, but this is exactly what the Horde is doing. He reluctantly picks up the katana.

"So, what do they call you in the halls of Hordsville High?" James asks.

The Horde laughs, clearly amused by the human. "I am Diriel, proud servant of Ageras of the East. And you, little man, are going to help me ascend."

"Never heard of you. But then again, my memory isn't what it used to be. I'm guessing I wouldn't know a piece of trash like you, let alone this Ageras."

CHAPTER 26

James takes a deep breath and sighs. "So, let's get that ascension of yours over with before your friend over there pulls himself together and beats you to it."

Diriel strides over to the pile of Horde remains, shaking the floor with each step. He lifts his massive foot and stomps down, pulverizing the Horde's body into the ground. Bone and other remains are forced out from beneath his foot. The crowd boos and laughs at the spectacle.

"So much for honour among thieves," James mutters to himself.

Chapter 27

The NLJ-010420 hovers five thousand feet above the town of Burns, Oregon. Its black exterior blends seamlessly with the night sky, making it nearly invisible to the naked eye. Advanced stealth technology ensures it eludes all known radar. In the cockpit, Aayaan waits patiently for the ground agents to report in, glancing anxiously at the fuel gauge. Secure refuelling sites are scarce after the attack on the Order, with many countries cutting ties or officially rejecting them. Thirty-five minutes ago, he dropped Helen, Scott, and the recently returned Watanabe a mile from the compound below.

The large private estate, resembling a fortified stronghold, is home to the Children of Sa-Chia. Local law enforcement is aware of the "cult" and attempts to monitor it, but budget cuts and a new administration have severely reduced their efforts. The Children of Sa-Chia, formed in 1910, worship what they believe to be their God and savoir and largely keep to themselves, emerging only to gather supplies or recruit new followers. Many families have been torn apart and lost loved ones to this cult. Unlike most groups, they have been visited by their savoir, Satanachia, a Horde entity with a peculiar appetite for elderly females, whom he uses to strengthen his followers.

CHAPTER 27

Helen, Scott, and Watanabe move stealthily from the compound's wall, dressed in black combat gear and carrying suppressed SIG Sauer XM7 assault rifles. The compound includes three huts used as dormitories, and the NLJ-010420 previously scanned heat signatures indicating ten people in each. At the compound's other end are garages, storage containers, and a large central building, likely a place of worship.

The three agents enter their respective huts and almost immediately exit from the other side. They use tranquillizer darts to secure the occupants with no resistance. However, upon regrouping, they notice several armed guards patrolling the perimeter.

"We need to get past them without being detected. This could turn into a firefight, and we don't have the time for that. Watanabe, you take point. I'll cover you both. My temperament for stealth is thin right now, and I could end up causing more harm than good."

Watanabe places a reassuring hand on Helen's shoulder and nods. He leads, with Scott following closely, as they move past a mechanic's garage with several jeeps, some in mid-repair. They freeze at the sound of a cough to their right, followed by a southern drawl.

"Ah tol' you to quit those things, Jonesy," followed by a loud spit.

"An' Ah tol' you to shut it, Stan," Jonesy snaps back.

A wheezing laugh from Stan is abruptly cut short by two silenced shots. The agents step over the bodies and reach the large grey concrete building in the compound's centre. They approach a side door, but Scott finds it locked. He listens carefully.

"Side door is locked. Moving to the front."

"Acknowledged," Helen replies, observing through her rifle scope from behind a jeep as the others move to the front.

At the large double doors at the front, Scott pauses to survey the perimeter before attempting the handle. He takes a deep breath, turns the unlocked handle, and pushes the door open just enough to slip inside. The room is shrouded in darkness, so Scott stops to the right of the door and removes his backpack. He pulls out two sets of night vision goggles, puts his own on, and taps Watanabe twice on the left wrist. Watanabe takes the goggles, puts them on, and sees Scott giving him a thumbs-up, which he returns. Watanabe signals Scott, who gives a thumbs-up in response. Scott double-clicks his ear.

"Go ahead," Helen's voice comes through the comms.

"We're inside. There are no lights, but we're sensing a Horde presence. It's oddly faint, though," Scott whispers.

"Oddly faint?" Helen asks, puzzled.

"Yes, it feels almost like a pulsing sensation. It's unlike anything we've experienced before."

CHAPTER 27

A creaking noise from the back of the room cuts Scott off.

"Stand by."

Helen does not respond.

The large room resembles a church with rows of pews, but instead of an altar, there is a large stone table. The table is stained with blood, and it appears to have never been cleaned. Old and new flowers are scattered on the floor around the table. Beside it is a wooden desk with several knives of varying shapes and sizes, all cleaned and ready. The agents move silently to either side of the room and approach the stone table, investigating the source of the noise. Behind the table, an old man sits slumped in a wooden chair, looking as if he has been mauled by a wild animal. His clothing is torn and soaked with blood. Scott moves closer and aims his weapon at the man's head. The man tries to smile at him.

"Don't move, or I'll turn your head into a canoe."

"You might want to take off your goggles," the man says with a strained voice.

Scott looks at Watanabe and then at the large floodlights on the ceiling. They both remove their night vision goggles just as the lights come on, illuminating the room. Scott raises his weapon again, and Watanabe covers the rest of the room. Four men with assault rifles enter, training their weapons on the agents.

"Don't move. Drop your guns," they shout repeatedly.

"I suggest you take a breath and calm down. You won't survive what comes next," Watanabe says.

The four men stop and exchange confused looks.

"What the hell does that mean? Listen, Bruce Lee, if you don't put your gun down, we'll kill you. Do you understand English?" one man demands, emphasizing each word.

"Enough. Put away your weapons. NOW," the old man shouts, coughing violently.

The men comply, lowering their AK-47s, and are startled by a voice behind them.

"You boys aren't as stupid as you look," Helen says.

They turn around, and Helen motions her rifle up and down—the universal sign to drop your weapon. They comply, raising their hands in surrender.

"Put your hands down; you're embarrassing yourself," the old man wheezes.

Helen ignores the men, walking past them up the aisle to stand next to Watanabe, who has also turned away from the men.

"Hello, Satanachia," Helen says to the old man.

CHAPTER 27

"How honoured I am to have three Agents of Solomon in my house, or should I say, former Agents of Solomon." Satanachia's laugh turns into a cough.

They do not react.

"Considering our Order has been completely decimated, we still look better than you," Scott says.

"Yes, I do look a bit worse for wear," Satanachia admits.

"You're not healing," Watanabe points out.

"No, and I won't. If you've come for information, I'm afraid you're in the dark. I've been stripped of my title, my legions, and my right to remain above ground."

They exchange glances. Watanabe looks at Helen, who tenses. He takes a step forward, prompting her to look at him. His slight shake of the head makes her relax.

"Every few hundred years, there's a change in management, and things get shuffled around. But with the recent discovery, everything is changing rapidly. Tabula Rasa approaches, and nothing will stop Her."

"Her, you mean Lilith?" Helen asks.

"So you are more informed than I thought," Satanachia says with a smile.

"What is the discovery?" Helen continues.

Satanachia's smile fades, and he shakes his head.

"Oh well, maybe you don't know as much as I thought."

"The dust," Watanabe says.

"This is quite the emotional roller coaster. If I had time, I'd explain everything to you, but alas, my time is running out. Nothing is what it seems, and allegiances are all a lie. The time of The Horde is coming, and nothing can stop the cleanse."

Satanachia laughs weakly before another coughing fit takes over. Helen raises her rifle, aiming at Satanachia's head. He lifts a finger.

"You've come all this way. I can give you something. Search for dead zones."

Helen fires three rounds into Satanachia's head, while Scott and Watanabe turn and shoot the men at the back. Helen's tattoos begin to glow as a wind picks up.

Ten minutes later, the NLJ-010420 accelerates away from the state, heading towards the Atlantic Ocean.

Chapter 28

James stands in the centre of the arena, blood and bits of Horde staining his torn and shredded clothing. His hair is matted with blood and sweat, some of it his own. His wounds have healed, but the symbols on his arms glow with an intense heat.

He has lost count of how many Horde he has defeated, or how many days he has been fighting. His nerve endings are on fire, and his heart races, almost too much for his chest to contain. Every time he defeats a Horde and tries to tap into the power he has, they find new ways to interrupt him expelling it. The power coursing through him feels like a drug, but he knows he cannot sustain this. Despite having been fed and allowed to sleep for brief periods, he has no sense of what day it is. He must keep fighting; there is no other option.

Curious, he lifts his arms to inspect his tattoos. They glow with an intense heat, almost like they have just been branded into him. The feeling is a strange mix of high and weakness, with energy pulsing through his arms and fingers.

His breathing is laboured, and he coughs up blood. There is something in the air, something that tastes like ash. They must have started pumping something from air vents. His eyes are stinging and as it lands on his skin, despite being too small to see he can feel it burning.

His thoughts are scattered, with memories he thought lost surfacing in a chaotic flood. He struggles to focus on the immediate threat. The lights around him begin to dance, signalling a new challenge.

A large figure enters from the top of the ramp, illuminated by the shifting lights. Paimon, bare and blue, strides down the ramp.

"Have you ever seen anything like this?" he bellows to the crowd, no microphone needed.

The crowd erupts with cheers and shouts. The gate to the arena opens, and Paimon enters with a shark-like grin.

"This has been a spectacle. Forget the gladiatorial games of Rome, forget the great battles of Carthage. This is the fight to end all fights."

He turns to James. "Still trying to catch your breath, I see."

Turning back to the crowd, Paimon continues, "But now it's time to change the rules. You've all enjoyed the warm-up, but now we come to the main event. Let's level the playing field."

Paimon gestures to a darkened section of the crowd that James has not noticed before. A dark figure sits on what can only be a

CHAPTER 28

throne. Paimon bows to the figure and then turns back to the crowd.

"Look upon our victory. Look upon our future."

James sees a smaller figure walking down the ramp, holding what looks like a bow. Paimon exits the arena but remains nearby.

James searches for the table where new weapons should have appeared, but it is absent. He scans the discarded weapons around him, broken or out of ammunition. As he looks up, an arrow slams into his left side, sending him sprawling to the floor. The crowd erupts.

James lies on the ground, waiting for the stars to clear from his vision. He sits up, pain radiating from the arrow lodged in his abdomen. He pulls out the fibre glass arrow, relieved that it has a bullet head and doesn't leave a large hole. Blood pours out, but something is wrong; he isn't healing, not even slowly.

Examining the arrowhead, he notices it is coated with something resembling charcoal or dust. James looks up and rolls to the side just as another arrow shoots past him, narrowly missing his head. Standing in the arena is Astaroth, smiling.

Ignoring the excruciating pain, James charges at Astaroth, who is pulling back his bow. James slams his shoulder into Astaroth, knocking the bow from his hands. He grabs Astaroth's jacket, twists it, and throws him over his shoulder, away from the discarded weapon.

James tries to stand straight, but the pain forces him to slump forward. He turns to the bow and, wincing with every breath, slowly picks it up. Astaroth stands up and starts to laugh.

"You okay there, James? You know, the last time I heard someone making that kind of noise was your daughter, as I slowly took my time with her."

James growls and charges forward, but Astaroth is ready. He dodges to the side and delivers a kick to the spot where the arrow struck. James collapses, sliding across the floor. The crowd cheers and barks with excitement. Astaroth crouches beside James.

"Hear that?" Astaroth pauses for effect. "That's the sound of your kind finally getting what they deserve. You seek revenge for some pathetic human you can't even remember, but we seek revenge for centuries of slaughter at your hands. We have the advantage now. You will die here tonight, James, and the rest of you will follow."

Astaroth stands and kicks James in the face and again in the gut, striking the open wound. He lifts James by the scruff of his neck and carries him like a doll across the arena. He drops James against the side, propped up against the metal enclosure. Astaroth walks over to the discarded bow and picks it up. He then removes an arrow from the quiver strapped to his back and places it in the bow.

James can't move, finding no strength in his arms or legs.

CHAPTER 28

"You are a weak coward, Astaroth. Waiting until the last minute to face me."

"Indeed."

THUNK

An arrow slams into James's left shoulder, and he lets out a painful cry. The crowd's cheers grow louder. His body stiffens as the pain erupts.

THUNK

Another arrow strikes his right knee. He tries to move, to escape, but the pain is overwhelming.

CLANG

An arrow misses his head and hits the metal arena behind him. The crowd laughs and taunts Astaroth, who ignores them. James's vision blurs, his head spins, and darkness closes in. The pain is relentless, and he is surprised he has lasted this long. The wounds are not healing, and the pain spreads through his body.

He looks forward and sees a blurry figure ahead, pulling back the bow, ready to release the arrow. Time seems to stop as he closes his eyes. The sound of cheers and laughter fades, and he slows his breathing, preparing for what's next. He has never feared death before, but now, faced with it, he can only think of one thing: Helen.

Memories flood his mind—memories of the woman he has loved since the dawn of time. They have lived many lives, with many names, but always together. He sees the life he shared with her and their beautiful daughter. A smile forms on his face as he feels a tear run down his cheek, knowing she will be his last thought.

BOOM.

An explosion erupts from Astaroth, throwing him sideways into the arena wall, pieces of him scattering. James turns his head and sees a figure landing on the floor, holding what looks like a grenade launcher. The figure runs over, kneels beside him, and throws the weapon aside.

"James?"

He feels the arrows being pulled from his body one by one, his body going limp. He is propped up into a sitting position.

"James, can you hear me?"

His eyes open slightly. Helen looks into his eyes and examines his wounds.

"Stay here and let the wounds heal. I'll buy you some time," Helen says.

She kisses him and stands, scanning the arena at the screaming, roaring crowd. There are too many Horde to count, all watching like the crowds at the Colosseum.

CHAPTER 28

"Well, this is a pleasant surprise," booms a deep voice.

Helen turns and sees Paimon through the fence of the arena. He leaps over the fence and lands with a thud. He raises his arms and opens his mouth, but before he can speak, Helen fires her last grenade into his torso, throwing Paimon back against the cage wall. As he struggles to recover, she drops the launcher, grabs a Heckler & Koch G36 assault rifle, and opens fire. Her shots hit Paimon's face and torso, and she reloads, firing again. Paimon roars and stumbles back, his face ripped open by the barrage of explosive rounds. Helen throws her rifle aside and charges at Paimon, who is reeling against the fence.

Before she reaches Paimon, Helen pulls out James's Billy Clubs from the holders on her shoulder blades and presses a button on each to electrify them. She strikes Paimon in the face twice to keep him off balance and kicks him in the chin as she flips backward. Jumping close, she hits his left knee, and as he falls, she shatters his jaw with a clubbed uppercut. Paimon lashes out blindly with razor-sharp claws, but Helen dodges effortlessly. She strikes the sides of his head with both clubs, electrifying his entire head before jumping back. She discards the now ruined clubs and pulls out two CZ 75 pistols from the holders at the small of her back. Before she can fire, a hand grabs the back of her jacket and throws her backward, causing her to hit the floor. Still holding the pistols, she corrects herself and springs to her feet.

Several Horde enter the arena, helping Paimon to his feet. Enraged by showing weakness, Paimon grabs a Horde to his left, squeezes its neck, and pushes the others away. He stands and growls at Helen, his throat too pulverized to speak.

The Horde in front of Helen ready themselves for an attack as she moves back toward James, who lies still on the floor. Concerned that he has not healed yet, she replies, "You didn't think our Lord wouldn't have us back him up, did you?"

"I wish I had thought of that," Helen says, squinting and smiling. "Oh wait, I did."

The wall to Helen's left explodes, sending large chunks of concrete into the crowd and crushing Horde as they land. Through the dust cloud, the nose of the NLJ-010420 hovers through the opening. The jet wobbles slightly but corrects itself, and two GUA-22/A Gatling Guns fire two hundred and twenty-two rounds from each barrel into the crowd. The guns move in different directions, hitting their targets with violent force.

The crowd is torn apart along with the seating and walls around them. Horde scramble to escape the firepower, with smoke rising from the demolished seating areas and screams coming from all directions. The jet moves back, the nose disappearing into the hole, but its weapons continue to carve a larger gap in the wall. The guns stop as the jet spins around, showing the rear doors opening. Two large harpoons with ropes attached fire from the jet and punch into the arena floor. Six figures slide down the ropes one at a time as the jet's engines roar, pulling the ropes and reversing out of sight.

Aayaan, Scott, Samantha, Watanabe, Billy, and Vlad stand

CHAPTER 28

ready, flanking Helen and James.

"What the hell is in the air?" Billy spits.

"Ignore it, we need to get James out of here." Helen advises.

They turn to James, covered in blood and looking terrible. He coughs up more blood and remains still. Helen examines the arrow wounds, confused.

"You're not healing." she says.

Fires have started in the crowd, and a large section of seating has collapsed due to the intense firepower. The room's structural integrity is failing, but no one is leaving. The Horde who can stand slowly move toward the arena, hungry and angry.

Paimon, now fully healed and covered in dust, pushes the Horde out of his way and glares at the Agents who have joined Helen. He shakes with anger, his humiliation too great to bear. There will be no conversation or gloating.

"Kill them all!" he roars.

The crowd responds with a deafening roar and charges into the arena. Aayaan fires his Saiga 12 into the faces of two Horde, exploding their heads. Watanabe unsheathe Sun-Nashi, a famous Tachi sword, and swiftly cuts three Horde into pieces before sheathing the sword and bowing to Aayaan, who smiles.

"I'm not having this again. You nearly caused a disaster last time you tried to outdo each other," Billy shouts at the two agents before pulling back his long brown coat and drawing his LeMat revolvers. The old Dodge City lawman fires the nine-shot pistols with precision at the oncoming Horde outside the arena, quickly reloading before the Horde crashes through the fences.

James opens his eyes and sees the battle raging in front of him. He cannot feel his body, but there is a pulsing sensation in his arms, the same feeling that has intensified with each purge. He notices something else as he looks at his wounds and the dust covering them.

He closes his eyes again and concentrates on the energy within him and the Horde around him. Memories long lost flood his mind—walking in the snow near the top of the Song Mountains in China, Shih urging him to breathe and let his Chi flow, Watanabe helping him meditate in Hōryū-ji, the laughter of Isla. Everything snaps into place.

"James," a voice calls from outside his memory.

"James, open your eyes for me."

He opens his eyes and sees a bruised and ruffled Helen holding his hand. James tilts his head, chaos unfolding behind her.

"Here was me thinking I looked bad," James smiles.

"We're in trouble, James. We need to get out of here. The Horde

CHAPTER 28

has done something. Vlad is dead, and Billy has a wound that isn't healing."

Helen looks at James's body. "You're also losing a lot of blood and will die if we don't leave."

"It's in the air and on their weapons." he replies.

Helen glances at the arrowhead in James's hand and then around the room, realization dawning on her. "The reactor. We're inside Chernobyl, next to the blown reactor. We thought they were using it to hide, but it's worse than we feared. They've weaponized the radiation."

Helen pauses. "We need to get up. Aayaan has signalled for Kenneth to bring back the jet, but the ceiling has closed the hole they came through. We need another exfil."

A loud bang to their left makes them look over to see Scott lying on the ground. Scott shakes his head, gets up, and charges toward a large Horde, disappearing into the chaos.

James stares at where Scott landed and notices two things: a belt with about ten frag grenades, which Scott must have dropped, and a broken, bloody Astaroth, who is moving slowly, trying to piece himself together but not seeing James or Helen.

"Help me get to my feet. I can be the distraction you need," James says.

"How? You're in no fit state..." Helen starts.

"Helen, look at me," James shouts. He lifts his arms, revealing his tattoos burning like white-hot electric fire. His pale skin is cracking, like clay, with the cracks spreading up his arms. "Whatever they've done to the air is affecting me more than just stopping me from healing. Every time I have used the power they have stopped me from releasing it. That energy is building, and I don't think I can stop it."

Helen opens her mouth to respond, but no words come out. James holds her face in his hands amidst the surrounding carnage. "I'm dying. I know that, but I think I can take out most of these things."

Tears fill Helen's eyes as she helps him to his feet, leaning him against the side and pulling him close for a hug. He whispers into her ear.

Astaroth, now kneeling and hearing the battle around him, looks up to see James in front of him. James feels nauseous and overwhelmingly dizzy, lacking the strength to move. He needs to make this count before Astaroth escapes. He doesn't have time to say anything and just smiles. He looks down, and the flames on his tattoos grow.

Everything in the arena stops. Slowly and painfully, James crosses his arms over his chest, and his tattoos erupt with white flames, flattening Astaroth to the floor. His arms spread out in a hug-like fashion in front of him. A blast wave of energy sweeps across the room, knocking everyone over. Energy and white fire engulf Astaroth as James creates a ball of energy in his arms. Lightning fires in all directions from the ball, striking

CHAPTER 28

and annihilating Horde in puffs of black smoke. A storm engulfs the stadium, pushing broken stadium pieces to the walls and crushing anything in its path. The ball transforms into something no one has ever seen—a singularity, a black hole.

Agents and Horde dodge lightning whips and debris as they move away from the ever-growing ball of light James holds. Astaroth disintegrates completely, but the energy continues to grow. James stands tall, arms outstretched, watching as the black hole pulls in Horde from every angle. Flashes of light fill his vision, like images from a camera, but he can't focus on them.

Paimon stares at the raw power and, with a final glance, leaps over the fence, disappearing through the doorway up the ramp, followed by several Horde. The Agents continue to fight the remaining Horde, but more try to escape, terrified of the singularity. The pull of the black hole draws in more than just Horde—pieces of seating and structure are sucked in and disappear, feeding the growing singularity.

James's skin cracks and burns away in white flames as the black hole pulses. Everything seems to move in slow motion as he turns his head toward Helen, who is outside the arena, avoiding dropping concrete and lightning. She feels his gaze on her.

She turns to James, who offers a smile. The others are with her: Aayaan carrying a lifeless Vlad. Kenneth and Scott helping Billy.

"I love you," she mouths to him.

She waits, absorbing his eyes one last time. She has loved him since the beginning of time and will continue to love him until the end. He smiles, breaking her trance.

Helen turns to the Agents, tears streaming down her face, and urges them to leave. They don't protest and quickly scramble up the ramp. Helen hears James's last words echo in her mind.

"I remember you now."

As they scurry over rubble and Horde, Samantha shouts into her radio but gets no response. They pass through a tall corridor, moving past security checkpoints and decayed control rooms. Scott throws a sticky bomb at a door, which explodes on impact.

"I'm going to her, Helen. I'm going to our daughter."

The Agents rush through the ruined door and exit onto waste ground just as the NLJ-010420 flies into view, screeching to a halt overhead. It lands in front of them, and as soon as the last Agent boards, the rear ramp closes, and the jet rockets away to safety.

"I'm going home." James's voice echoes in Helen's mind.

Inside the arena, the singularity James holds is overwhelming. His skin, burnt across most of his body, exposes muscle and bone in places. Suddenly, everything goes silent. His body

CHAPTER 28

turns numb as the storm and lightning vanish. His body heals instantly, the pain disappears, and he emanates a brilliant, white light as if radiating from every pore like the sun. Flashes of images come into his vision, clearer than ever before.

He sees himself standing in the Glasgow facility, staring at old photographs of Helen and their daughter.

He is in their old flat, a week ago, looking at Helen and Pete before going to the art gallery.

Five years ago, he is picking up a scared and injured young Pete, escaping before the police arrive.

In 1975, he shouts at Helen and a younger Miles, feeling deep loss and anger.

In 1948, he holds their child for the first time, passing her to Helen as they rescue her from a massacre.

In 1815, he aims his rifle at the advancing forces and fires.

In 480 BC, he stands shoulder to shoulder with his brothers and sisters as the Persians charge.

In 3200 BC, he holds Helen in his arms, watching a boat with sails glide down the Nile.

In 30,000 BC, he stands over the body of the tribe leader, his blood on his hands.

James snaps back to the present, he hears a voice—or rather, he feels a voice in his ear.

"Let go, Dad."

He closes his eyes, letting go of the visions, and is engulfed by light. The jet banks around, passing over the site of the greatest nuclear disaster in history. It explodes in a blinding flash. A cloud of white fire rises into the sky, expanding over a 19-mile radius. The devastation engulfs the area for over a minute before fading away.

Kenneth and Aayaan grip the controls with all their strength, pulling the jet up and away from the cataclysmic event.

Chapter 29

Two months have passed since the destruction of the Eastern European Nuclear Power Plant. What was once a scar on the landscape is now a crater stretching 1,000 square miles and half a mile deep. Within days, plant life not previously seen in the area—or even the country—began to grow in and around the crater, bringing a resurgence of wildlife.

The area is now covered in an inch of snow, a rarity due to the radiation that once filled the air. Radiation levels are now undetectable. Helen, bundled in winter clothing but with her head and face exposed, stands at the edge of the crater, watching snow fill the void. Her red curls blow in the wind, and her face is flushed from the cold. She crouches, scraping away some snow to reveal a smooth, reddish stone that seems out of place in this part of the world. She turns it over in her hands, and gazes up at the sky.

A horn sound pulls her from her reverie. She turns to see a black van with tinted windows parked a few yards behind her, stark against the white landscape. Taking one last look at the crater, she walks over to the van and slides open the side door. Inside, Scott is seated in the driver's seat, wearing a bright red snowboarding jacket and an orange woolly hat, looking cold. The back of the van is fitted with top-of-the-line surveillance and communication equipment. Pete sits at the main computer, with only his eyes visible through his thick parka, ski trousers, and winter boots. Helen looks at Scott, who nods to Pete.

Pete mumbles something through the layers of his clothing. Helen tilts her head and gives him a questioning look. He drops his shoulders, fumbles with his gloves, pulls down his snood, and tries again.

"He's made contact and isn't happy about having to wait."

"We wouldn't want him to be unhappy now, would we?" Helen replies with evident sarcasm as she steps inside the van and closes the door. She sits in the chair behind the front passenger seat and nods to Pete, who presses a few keys on his computer.

"I'm here," Helen says.

"About bloody time. Waiting isn't in my nature, nor is talking to your assistant," a male voice comes through the speaker above Pete.

Pete opens his mouth to respond, but Helen raises a hand and gives him a look of understanding.

"You can either spend the remaining ninety seconds before the trace completes complaining to me, or you can get to the point."

CHAPTER 29

A five-second silence follows before the voice breaks it.

"He's in Taranto."

Pete quickly works his computer, bringing up a map on the large screen. Scott chimes in before Pete.

"It's in Italy, near the heel," he says smugly.

Pete scowls at Scott as Helen rolls her eyes.

"Well done, you own a map," says the speaker.

Before Scott can protest, Helen cuts him off.

"You can confirm he's in Italy?"

"Yes."

"How accurate is your intelligence?" Helen presses, leaning forward in her seat.

"I have my hand wrapped around his throat."

Helen glances at Scott, who can't help but smile, but the voice isn't finished.

"Say hello, Astaroth," followed by a gurgling sound.

"We're leaving now. Send the address, and we'll be with you in about thirty hours."

"I'll be here."

"Valac?"

"I'm still here," Valac responds.

"Thank you."

A click sounds, indicating the call has ended. Helen slumps back into her seat and exhales deeply. She waits for about a minute, feeling the others' eyes on her, waiting for her to give the order. She finally does.

"OK, let's go."

Printed in Dunstable, United Kingdom